Damron

THE SHAPE
OF
ILLUSION

THE SHAPE
OF
ILLUSION

William E. Barrett

Doubleday & Company, Inc.

Garden City, New York

CONTENTS

For
Louis and Matilda
James and Anne
Vincent and Charline
Albert and Juanita
Edward and Sonia

BOOK ONE
The Painting

CHAPTER ONE

There was no reason why I should not be a painter of note, one of those riding high and comfortably on the wave of public interest in art and artists. I was twenty-nine and I had done my time in Europe and I knew what to do with brushes and paint and canvas. My disqualification in the race to glory and the rich rewards was of my own creation or my own temperament. I did not paint abstractions or the essence of anything, nor landscapes nor portraits; I painted heads and faces. I painted the kind of faces that surround the entrances of old cathedrals or that look at one from beneath the pulpits inside the cathedrals; strong faces and, for the most part, masculine faces. One does not become a famous artist with an obsession like that, but one is shackled to one's obsessions.

I was doing the sketch of a head from memory when the phone rang, the head of a man who sold vegetables a few blocks from my studio. It was a head and face that belonged in another century and in another place. I did not care which century or which place. The phone rang urgently and, reluctantly, I answered it.

The voice of Ludwig Lorenson came over the wire to

me. "Kirk," he said, "is it convenient for you to come to the studio? The next half hour? I have something to show you. There will be a few other people."

"I'll come. Certainly," I said.

Ludwig Lorenson always disconcerted me, always made me awkward in speech and in response. Ludwig Lorenson is a dealer in abstractions. The thought does not immediately occur to one because the Lorenson Galleries are not a castle in Spain; they are an institution of solid value, housed in a substantial building which was designed to contain, to protect, and to exhibit objects of tangible reality.

Traffic was heavy and the cab consumed a half hour in conveying me to the galleries. As I crossed the sidewalk toward the main entrance, I narrowly missed a collision with Rabbi Gerson Marler who was making an angry exit. He looked at me and, if he saw me, he did not recognize me. The lines and wrinkles in his face were set in cement and he walked away from Lorenson's with a swift, jerky stride. I had known him for several years. He had a great capacity for indignation, a vast amount of impatience, under the normally placid surface of genial, scholarly good nature; but the explosive quality was a dramatic outlet and not bad temper. Drama was integral to his personality. I had seen him angry on other occasions but never blind angry.

Ludwig Lorenson, too, had been out of the norm. I had been present one fall day at an auction where Ludwig Lorenson had bid the highest price ever paid for a painting in the United States and his voice had been as perfectly controlled as if he were ordering lunch. Today he had been excited or disturbed; there had been emotion in his voice.

The interior of the Lorenson Galleries was austere and

serene, entirely normal, with no marks of altercation or angry passage. Robert, the elderly colored man who operated the elevator, wore his usual smile of welcome as he greeted me. For customers, or clients, of Ludwig Lorenson there were only three floors to the galleries; for certain friends of Ludwig's there were four. Conversations with Robert were necessarily short, a serial story, always continued in the next installment.

"How's the new chauffeur making out, Robert?" I asked.

"Badly, Mr. Donner." He shook his head. "That man's lazy. Dust all over my Cadillacs every morning."

"That's what I hear everywhere. People don't take their work seriously any more. You'll have to fire him."

"I've been considering it. That's a bad decision."

We had talked in that vein for several years, straight-faced and without levity. It was Robert's own legend and he had taught me to play up to it. He had a spinal injury and was capable of no more demanding work than this seemingly simple task of pressing buttons, but he brought dignity to the task and gave it stature. He knew how to meet the people who came to Lorenson's; the mighty, the almost-mighty, and the preposterous. With fourth-floor visitors he relaxed. I had heard many times of his problems with his yachts and his Cadillacs and his investments in Wall Street, anecdotes told with amazing twists and with flashes of irony, but of his actual problems, the realities of his life, the trouble that he must have had, and the pain, I knew nothing. A dusty Cadillac is amusing and trouble is not. It was part of his wisdom to understand that.

I was one of the few people, I believe, who knew that Robert's name was Maxwell. The year that I discovered his name, I painted a portrait of him from memory and seated

him behind the wheel of an old Maxwell automobile.
The painting was a Christmas gift, but I made a gift to
myself in the giving of it. It made me one of Robert's
special people.

The elevator door opened on Ludwig's study, a dark-
paneled Florentine room of many books but with only
one painting. The painting, however, was a luxury and an
extravagance, the portrait of an attractive scoundrel by
Antonello da Messina. Ludwig was waiting for me, not
engrossed in work at his desk nor at ease with a book, but
arrested in the act of room-pacing.

"Ah, Kirk," he said, "it was good of you to come on
such short notice. I am glad that you are here before the
others. Did you see Rabbi Marler?"

"I did. He didn't see me."

"He was upset. Come! I have something remarkable to
show you."

Ludwig opened a door on his right and led the way,
with speed if not grace, down a long passage; a slender
soul, a fastidious spirit, propelling an uncouth, oddly made,
awkward body with which it was burdened. He snapped a
light switch in the large, monastically severe room that I
knew well, the room in which he exhibited certain pictures to carefully selected people. He took a half-dozen
steps and turned so that he could watch my face. I
was aware of him for the moment, then no longer aware of
him.

The cleverly contrived lighting suspended a large canvas in space so that there seemed to be no other life, or
being, or inanimate thing, in the room with it. It was an
old canvas with vertical streaks, like bars of faded soot, near
the edges on either side. It had been cleaned but not re-
cently. There were a number of cobweb cracks in the

paint and some flaking where the paint had been built up
to develop shadow. The central area was little damaged,
lightly filmed with grime and dust since the cleaning. The
painting had been spared long exposure to sunlight or the
destructive smoke of votive candles, so that it was remarka-
bly preserved. All of this was a momentary impression;
mental comment, made and dismissed. I stood in a practically nonexistent room and looked into the courtyard of
Pontius Pilate's palace some two thousand-odd years ago.

The Christ had been scourged and exhibited to the
people, Pilate had washed his hands, and the Roman soldiers were taking Jesus through the courtyard where they
would, presently, load upon his shoulders the cross upon
which he was to die. First, however, they must reckon with
the mob. Men, women, and children, wealthy and poor,
blocked the way, howling their hatred at the dazed man
who stood within the circle of Roman soldiery. They were
shouting, spitting, and hurling stones, those people, and
the Romans were endeavoring to force them back. The
foreground figure, a magnificent soldier, was pressing
against them with the buckler on his left arm, the muscles
of his legs and arms rigid.

Jesus Christ, in a white robe stained with blood, stood
with his legs well apart, standing upright with obvious
effort. He had been heavily punished and the marks of his
punishment were on him. There was blood in his hair,
running down over his forehead, and his mouth was cut.
His shoulders were hunched slightly forward as though
he sought to draw his lashed back away from contact
with his robe. He was looking into the faces before him
and it was difficult to read his expression. He seemed dazed
but his eyes were alive. They did not mirror fear, nor

hatred, resentment or surprise; they were, perhaps, merely asking a question.

I drew a deep breath, reminding myself that this was merely a painting, that its compelling sense of reality was due, in great part, to Ludwig's superb staging.

"Magnificent!" I said. "An amazing find. Who is it?"

Ludwig's voice out of the shadows was slightly hoarse, edged with impatience. "No. No. The artist does not matter. He was a nobody. You never heard of him."

"Impossible. The man who painted that was no unknown. He couldn't be."

I was looking at the painting now with my other pair of eyes, no longer aware of the human drama, the man at bay, aware only of how this miracle of illusion had been wrought on canvas. The work was unquestionably German, but it suggested Tintoretto or, in its portraiture, Caravaggio.

Who else but Tintoretto would have had the daring to place a minor figure of the drama so commandingly in the foreground as was that thrusting Roman? It was the same daring that had placed a superb, full-bodied woman on the foreground steps while the tiny figure of the Virgin climbed at right angles to her in his great "Presentation."

"You are not observing the details," Ludwig said.

Was I not? The angry crowd formed a semicircle at the lower left, balanced by an arc of dark, tumbling cloud, a low hill and Pilate's balcony on the upper right, with the solitary figure of Christ in the exact center of the diagonal, but not seeming to be. The massed human figures shortened the foreground while the placing of the balcony and the hill, on either side behind the central figure, gave perspective to the clouds, creating the impression of deep space. It was midmorning after a night of rain, with puddles in the cracked tiles of the courtyard. The light flowed feebly into the painting from behind the beholder, touching the mob with only enough strength to reveal it, gaining its greatest strength where it illumined the figure of Christ, resting wanly at last against the marble pillar beneath the balcony and the rough stone of the wall.

"Look at the people!" Ludwig said.

One does not see all of a great painting at a glance, nor in a few moments. One progresses from the general to the particular according to one's temperament and one's interests. I was not ready for the mob, but I gave them my attention when Ludwig demanded it.

They were people whipped to a fury of hatred and denunciation. There was movement in them and tension. They shouted and spat and brandished fists, swore no doubt, and reached for bits of jagged stone where the pavement had cracked under the hoofs of horses. The Renaissance painters did their own people and set them down in the Holy Land, Egypt, Ancient Greece, or wherever their imaginations led them. This artist had been a German, you could tell that from his people. The artists of that school were portrait painters, or all of the good ones were. Their masses, or groups, always resolve themselves into sharply defined individuals when you study them. I studied this mob now, fewer people actually than there appeared to be.

Immediately, I saw myself.

I was in the third row of those who were being hurled back by the Roman with the outthrust buckler. I had taken one step away from the pressing front lines to bend over in search for a missile to throw. My fingers were closing around a jagged piece of stone that was not quite

so large as the hand which sought it. I seemed to be
muttering something.

It was no mere resemblance; it was a portrait. I have
shaved my own face often enough to know its every contour and this was neither an older "I" nor a younger, it
was myself as I was. The mood was not a familiar one
because I am not normally given to hatred or violence
or running with human packs, but the face was mine
and I had to accept the vicious purpose with which it
was stamped. In the moment of that acceptance, I felt
the emotion, fleeting but disturbing, the urge to reach, to
grasp, to destroy. I turned to Ludwig.

"I see it," I said. "Did you bring me here to see myself,
or the painting?"

Ludwig was noticeably tense, but no longer impatient
now that he was no longer called upon for patience. "You
and the painting are inseparable," he said. "I promise
you surprises. There is more on that canvas than paint
and varnish."

My eyes returned to the painting but it was distorted
for me now, out of balance and perspective. I saw only
that one furtive, cowardly figure. There was a child a
few feet to the right who was also reaching for a piece
of stone, reaching with greater agility than I, a freer
sense of movement and purpose in his limbs, instinctive
in action rather than meanly cruel. Looking at the scene,
I could not escape a sense of identification with the man
who wore my face, and I resented the child because his
duplication of my action convicted me of a childish act.
I was less forthright than those who swore and shouted
and brandished fists.

"How can this be?" I said. "This painting is no crude
pistache by a forger. I refuse to believe that it was done

by a contemporary who included my portrait as a jest. Yet, that is I! Unmistakably."

"It is as old as it appears to be; seventeenth century. The artist, as I said, was nobody. A man named Rohlmann: Boniface Rohlmann. There is, I assure you, no shadow of a jest connected with it."

Ludwig was unwontedly solemn and when I looked at him, his eyes were fixed intently upon the painting. He had little color in his skin even when, on rare occasions, he sought sunlight, but his pallor was more heavily laid on today and the pallor of a large, full-faced man has an arresting quality.

"Reincarnation?" I ventured tentatively. "I do not believe in it, but . . ."

"No. No." Ludwig interrupted me, substituting his limping, half-coherent phrases for my hesitant, half-completed sentence. "If one lived more than once, we would not possess the same faces in different centuries. That could not be. Changing times, changing faces; customs, environment, mixtures of blood. Consider the great portraits! No. That is no answer at all."

A gentle bell proclaimed the fact that the elevator was starting its ascent with another visitor for the fourth floor. Ludwig hurried away with a word of apology, relieved, I am certain, to escape from a discussion that had drifted into strange and awesome paths. I forced myself to consider the painting once more, simply as a painting, not dwelling upon the figures. My attention leaped to a detail. The balcony of Pontius Pilate was empty. A lesser painter than this one would have placed a watching Pilate there, if only as a symbol. This man knew better. Pilate would not have been there. As a symbol that empty balcony was eloquent.

Voices echoed in the passageway as the door opened. Ludwig was leading Neil Carlton into the room. We greeted each other with the easy informality of those who meet often. Neil was an ordained minister but he had laid aside the "Reverend" in all but formal contacts when he assumed the editorship of a leading Protestant review. He was a medium tall, distinguished man with a clipped red-brown mustache, heavy gray eyebrows, and mild eyes; a keen observer rather than a militant crusader. Literature and music were his fields rather than painting, but I often met him in the galleries where his taste seemed to incline to the moderns.

"This painting must be indeed special, granting your urgency full weight, Ludwig," he said. "Ah! I see that it is. One of your discoveries! A Renaissance."

He removed from their case the glasses that he wore for distant viewing, adjusting them carefully, leaning forward slightly. "Wonderful! Astounding reality. It makes one a spectator. Where?"

His voice broke sharply and his tall figure leaned several degrees more toward the canvas. He removed his glasses and walked to within a couple of feet of it. He stood for a full minute frozen into immobility, then he turned around and there was shock in his face.

"You should have prepared me for this, Ludwig," he said. "To discover myself in such a scene and in such a role! One should not walk in upon it. One should be steeled."

He sat in one of the chairs that were placed in an arc at viewing distance from the painting and there was an element of collapse in his manner of seating himself. For a man so poised and unruffled in the ordinary course of affairs, this sudden falling apart was horrible. Obviously, he had discovered himself in the painting as I had, and the discovery was a deeper emotional experience to him than to me. He was a minister in that moment of discovery, neither editor nor detached observer, nor casual patron of the arts.

"I am sorry, Neil," Ludwig was saying.

My eyes passed slowly over the faces of the mob and I could not find Neil Carlton, nor anyone who suggested Neil Carlton in feature, expression, or attitude; yet somewhere in that mass, he had discovered himself. It was then that I realized, although as yet dimly, that we were confronted by something that had terror in it.

The ringing of the silver bell that announced another fourth-floor visitor was like the Sanctus bell in the old Mass, a solemn announcement of an impending portentous event. An experience not of this world awaited the guest who was ascending in the elevator and he did not know it. I, who did know, felt suspense as an activity rather than as a passive waiting, a crawling of nerves under my skin. I glanced at my two companions. Neil Carlton's face was white and he was staring at the canvas. He was not aware that his participation in the scene before him was shared. Ludwig was hesitating, his eyes on the doorway to the passage, obvious reluctance to repeat an experience written upon his features. He shook his shoulders violently, almost the shudder of sudden awakening, and moved forward, hurrying to atone for his hesitation.

Father Joseph Graney made his entrance cheerfully, relating some traffic-delay anecdote to Ludwig, the tone of his voice conveying the humor which belonged to words lost in the passageway. He was in his fifties, of medium height, beginning to put on a little weight which he did not have when I first knew him; round-faced, keen-eyed,

with a fringe of gray hair around the bald spot which
had been expanding in area during recent years. He was
a member of the faculty at the Jesuit university and he
had a solid reputation in art circles. He was the author of
a charming little volume on Duccio and an impressive
tome on the School of Siena.

Neil Carlton rose from his chair as Father Graney and
I were shaking hands. He had recovered his poise and we
visited for a few minutes, four people who shared many
interests and who met often in the sharing of them. Father
Graney detached himself from the conversation with a gesture.

"I am like the man who came late to the cocktail party,"
he said. "You have all been drinking this surprise of Ludwig's and I must catch up with you."

He walked to the center of the room and I watched his
face, projecting myself into him as best I could, trying
to see the painting with him and through him, establishing
myself emotionally for the inevitable climax.

Father Graney met the painting much as I did, seeing
it as a painting before he permitted himself to be drawn
to the content; but he passed through that preliminary
stage in less time than I. The figure of Christ caught and
held him. His face tightened, almost a wince, and that
was a tribute to the artist. As priest and art connoisseur,
the Jesuit was familiar, one would say to the point of
saturation, with every conceivable detail of the story before
him, but he did not look unmoved upon that dazed, beaten
figure, braced with the effort of holding his body upright
in the face of hatred, hostility, and abuse. His hands were
clasped behind his back and I saw his fingers move, loosen
their intertwined grip, then tighten. He reached the mob
then, without the prompting that I needed, pausing for a

moment to contemplate the Roman—leaning forward, almost lunging, as he discovered himself.

He wasn't there, of course; not to any eyes but his own. I had searched that painting for his face before he entered the room, certain that I would not find it but equally certain that he would.

We were enfolded within an unnatural quiet. The priest broke it, releasing his arrested breath in an angry snort. He turned away from the painting and walked to the rear of the room, obviously seeking control over himself in minor, meaningless action before trusting himself to speak. He spoke harshly when he did speak, walking back from the wall.

"I cannot believe, Ludwig," he said, "that you approve, or consider amusing, the vicious taste of the restorer who painted my portrait into that picture, or that you invited me here to see it in the presence of my friends."

Ludwig was distressed. There was sweat on his broad face, and that sweat which appeared so often at inopportune times was another of his personal crosses; a pitiless incongruity in a man whose impeccable mind had no coarseness. His right hand moved almost imperceptibly, a gesture of protest that died when it was still an impulse.

"The painting has never been restored," he said quietly. "It is authentically seventeenth century."

Father Graney stared at him belligerently for a moment, a reflex of action in a man who is angry and who does not recover immediately; then he wheeled toward the painting with that peculiar lunging motion of his. The painting itself stopped him in midlunge. It had not been restored, of course, and he knew that when he looked at it again. He had known it, undoubtedly, when he first looked at the painting, but a mind that is trained to logical thinking imposes logic upon the evidence of the senses even when the senses refuse support to the logic. There was no other sane explanation for his portrait in that screaming mob than the one which his mind supplied. He stood frozen now with the sane explanation reduced to vapor.

"I'm sorry, Ludwig," he said, "you are correct. I leaped to a conclusion. But the resemblance! It is more than a resemblance. It is appalling."

He spoke as you would imagine an automaton speaking, pumping out the words. Neil Carlton was beside him in one swift movement.

"Do you mean to say that your portrait is there, too?" he said incredulously. "Where? I do not see it."

He was adjusting his glasses. Father Graney looked at him suspiciously, as though he suspected him of pretending not to see the obvious. "What do you mean, 'too'?"

They were both intent upon the canvas and I studied the crowd again, trying to see it as they were seeing it, ignoring the furtive creature who was myself. There were three Romans. The soldier at the far edge of the crowd, on the viewer's left, was blurred and indistinct due to a long sooty streak in the canvas and some cobweb cracking in the paint. The people in this section were shadowy but there were several women among them, one of them carrying a child in her arms. The faces of three women and five men were clearly defined in the middle section, identifiable if one knew them. The Roman soldier who stood against them was merely a head under a helmet but he seemed to be having a difficult time. The surge of people had forced him to give ground. In the foreground, the faces were remarkable, the bodies solid but swept off balance by the powerful thrust of a youthful soldier. All Rome, and the might of it, was in that solitary figure. His weight was forward behind the buckler which he used as a ram and his left arm was a study in corded muscle as he pressed it against the resisting flesh. His right arm was held out from his body and bent. His right hand held a short sword but he seemed to be balancing his body with it rather than threatening. His face was brutish, unintelligent, betraying no emotion. He had a job to do and he had encountered an obstacle. He was removing the obstacle, neither thinking about it nor caring.

"That is I, that tall scoundrel in the crimson robe. Surely, you must see it!"

Neil Carlton's voice was like a voice from another world, so absorbed was I. Father Graney was slow in replying. "I see no resemblance," he said. "None whatever."

"Nor can I find anyone who remotely resembles you."

"Can't you? Well, look then at that vile creature spitting at his Lord and Saviour!"

There was deep feeling in the priest's voice and I could understand it because I had been unable to avoid self-identification with the despicable creature who was recognizably myself. Following Father Graney's pointing finger, I granted him the right to even a greater feeling of repulsion than my own; as a man, leaving his priesthood out of it, as one couldn't, of course. The figure to which he pointed was indeed vile, a hunched figure in rough and dirty clothing who was on the extreme tip of the crowd arc. He had slipped behind the soldier and was spitting at the lonely figure of Christ.

"Spitting," Father Graney repeated.

I do not know why spitting is worse than cursing, calling for a man's blood, reaching for a rock to throw at him, or brandishing fists; but it is, or seems to be. I looked at the figure in the crimson robe.

Neil Carlton, I thought, had fared better than had we. This man was tall, commanding, a personage, probably a Pharisee. His face was contorted with hatred and he was obviously shouting abuse but he was not stooping to stone or to spit. Almost immediately then, I saw him as Neil must have seen him and he seemed no better than the others. He had stooped, and stooped far enough, in surrendering his dignity, his reason, his intelligence, making himself one with a violent, ignorant rabble, a leader of the community howling like an animal, one of a lynch mob.

"I am not proud, either," I said.

I identified myself for them in the scene and we went through the pointless, repetitive routine of looking once more at the faces. Ludwig's voice, quietly controlled now, took command of us.

"We have, it seems, a serious matter to discuss. I suggest that we discuss it comfortably."

No one answered him. We seated ourselves in the chairs that faced the painting, but our comfort was questionable. We had been humbled in the contemplation of self and there is no comfort in that unless one is a mystic. Of the four of us, Neil was the most nearly relaxed. His mind had been challenged by an intellectual problem and that challenge steadied him. He thrust his long legs straight out and contemplated his shoes, his fingers locked into an arch that supported his chin.

"If I did not know you so well, Ludwig," he said, "I would say that this serious matter adds up to the fact that you have been dabbling in hypnotism like that chap, what's-his-name, who wrote Bridie Murphy. I feel as though I had witnessed the Indian rope trick, knowing that it did not happen, but still convinced that I saw it."

Ludwig gestured ponderously, shifting his heavy body. "If there is hypnotism, it is painted into the picture," he said gravely. "I know little of the painter except that he was unfortunate. The painting has caused trouble on the few occasions when it was exhibited and several attempts have been made to destroy it. It was protected by people who did not understand it, but who respected art and books and all learning. If we, who are in this room, cannot understand it, no one can."

"Such things as this are of the devil," Father Graney said.

"Or of God."

Ludwig's voice was challenging and the priest raised his head to look at him. "How, of God?"

"If good comes of it, if the message of the picture serves our better nature, then it is not evil."

"It is not so simple. The immediate effect may seem good, blinding us to an ultimate evil. That is true in many affairs."

"Consider!" Ludwig, who had urged upon us the desirability of comfort in discussion, was on his feet, a man who, when standing, was the picture of discomfort, robbed of dignity and repose by his ungainly contours. He gestured awkwardly toward the picture. "We are confronted with a terrible moment in the history of the world. Why is it terrible?"

We each had an individual answer to that, I suppose, but we waited for him to answer his own question. He was not himself. He could be suave, urbane, certain of his own good taste, confident in a vast cultural lore that

he had acquired and in the instincts that he had developed
in the acquiring; but he was without his resources today.
He could say much by speaking little and he never made
speeches on his feet, but here he was; sweat on his face,
moved by some torturing emotion, spouting rhetoric.

"This scene I have never encountered before in art,"
he said. "So many painters have done the 'Ecce Homo'
that I cannot count them in my mind; the Christ has been
flogged and Pilate shows him to the people. This scene
before us, nobody has done and nobody has written about.
It has a verity. They must have led him out through the
courtyard after Pilate washed his hands. The crowd would
be still there. A crowd, if it is angry, does not disperse.
This artist saw truly. The truth of fact is in the painting.
Is that not so?"

"It is a reasonable sequence of events," Father Graney
said.

Neil Carlton nodded imperceptibly. "There are natural
inferences in the Bible narratives, bridges of detail that
we may assume as connecting events. This is one, certainly."

They were sorry for Ludwig, I thought, somewhat embarrassed for him because he was playing an unaccustomed
role badly, and they were trying to help him. Still, they
were slightly withdrawn, opposed to him in some subtle,
if not actual, way. I did not say anything. I do not believe in helping people under such circumstances because
they usually do better without help. I was anticipating a
climax. Ludwig did not suffer over such innocuity as he
had expressed; he was suffering because of words that
were still unsaid.

"So," he said, "here or there, one time or another,
these people are shouting the most unfortunate words that

people ever spoke or shouted. They are saying: 'His blood be upon us and upon our children!' For this saying, my own people have suffered through twenty centuries. It has spilled oceans of blood, that saying, but it was not the saying of Jews only. You are not Jews, but you are there. You have seen yourselves."

Neil Carlton had drawn in his extended legs. He was sitting upright. "It has always been Christian doctrine," he said, "that Christ died for all, that we were all involved in his death and responsible for it."

Ludwig stood silent, looking at him, and there was weary skepticism in his face. Father Graney stirred. He ran his hand over his head and down the back of his neck.

"We teach, and have always taught," he said gruffly, "that every man who has ever sinned had a role in the crucifixion, that our sins nailed our Saviour to the cross. We display the crucifix to remind man of that."

"It is pious," Ludwig said, "but it is not the body of the doctrine. We Jews have been called 'Christ-killers' and confined to ghettos where we were few and you were many. The Good Friday services today keep that old hatred fresh."

"The Jews are not always zealous, either in writing or in preaching, to apply healing ointment and bandages to wounds," Father Graney said mildly.

The priest was staring at the painting. I could not imagine that Ludwig had said anything that had any novelty for him. He must have studied, debated, and meditated upon this question of guilt countless times during his long course of Jesuit studies, his career as an educator, but he did not draw upon the arsenal of argument that was undoubtedly his to answer that charge about "the body of the doctrine." It might be that he was sympathetic to Ludwig personally, his friend of many years, or that he recognized a sad truth in his friend's words, or that he found himself in the presence of a great abstraction made concrete on the canvas before him. I did not know.

Ludwig sat down heavily. He had spoken as he was not accustomed to speaking and he could not continue. "I do not understand this painting," he said, "nor how it was wrought, but it portrays a great truth. I feel it. It is on the side of justice."

Neil Carlton murmured something. I did not hear what he said. He rose abruptly and left the room. I noted the fact but, if I thought about it at all, I assumed that he had gone to the lavatory. I had joined my two companions in the silence of contemplation, than which there is no silence that more completely blots out the world.

We were seated on a low east wall of the courtyard, slightly above and behind the struggling crowd, with the pale morning sun at our backs. That was the focus of the picture and the direction of the light that flowed into it. It was a chilly day in Jerusalem with the wind blowing out of the northwest where the black clouds were heavily massed, an arc of menace as threatening as the packed humans below. One could see the wind in the puddles left by the night's rain, the slight ripple in them, and I thought again of Tintoretto. How he could make water flow on canvas! One could see the wind, too, in the garments of the people if one looked closely. It was plucking at them, not a strong wind but with a chill damp in it that would make itself felt.

Jesus was feeling it, standing alone in the middle of the courtyard. My first impression of him changed. That odd effect that he created, of shrinking away from the touch of his garments, was, in part at least, the effect of the wind as it touched the lacerations on his back, doubly chilling after the fever induced by frightful punishment.

That figure of the Christ dominated the scene when one viewed it whole. He was not compelling physically. His body was that of an ordinary man who has lived much in the out-of-doors, neither soft nor emaciated, nor developed for swift and sudden violence as was that of the Roman soldier. His face was marred by the streaks of blood. The dazing effect of the beating that he had received was expressed in a sagging of the facial muscles. At this moment, he was not at his best; but, as a spectator, I was held by him. The other figures, limned in dramatic action while he stood passive, were relatively unimportant. *He* was the painting, its *raison d'etre*.

He was invincible. That shouting rabble had not robbed him of his nobility, nor would they. They could not degrade him unless he joined them; they could only degrade themselves. As one of the degraded, within the circle and yet apart, I was baffled by the expression in the eyes of Christ. I had interpreted it as a question, but that was not it. He was not looking into the faces of his self-proclaimed enemies with hatred or resentment or defiance, the more apt descriptive word seemed to be regret, regret that we, who could aspire to lofty heights, had fallen low. Or, it was, perhaps, compassion, the knowledge that some day, in some place, we would stand helplessly as he stood and look upon ourselves, and be compelled to suffer the looking.

I do not, ordinarily, think such thoughts.

Emotion moved in me against my will, in actual combat with my will. I had put emotion behind me, banished it from my life, during the grim weeks when my wife was going through the ugly processes of divorce. I had prided myself that I could be detached, a commentator or observer of life rather than a participant in emotional absurdity. The painting challenged that self-assurance, challenged it with no help from implanted religious ideas. I had grown up in a mildly religious family, churchgoers of habit rather than of conviction. I had never been swept up, as many were, in the religious legends, traditions, and folklore. I walked away from all of it with finality in my freshman year at the university. The painting not only drew me into an old legend, it drew me into human hysteria, into suffering, into the weather of Jerusalem twenty centuries ago. All of which was absurd!

I shook my head, willing myself not to be a mere helpless spectator, summoning my other pair of eyes, the eyes of a painter. The Christ still commanded me. The hapless soldier, unable to hold his segment of the crowd, was the point of a wedge, an arrow pointing to that quiet, lonely figure. The foreground Roman, bracing his weight against humanity, was balancing himself with his sword arm and the sword point was another arrow indicating Christ. The wind blew toward him and the shaping of the clouds indicated him, and the light! The painter had not given him a glory, but he did not need it. The thin light of a cold, storm-heavy morning was barely enough to light the scene, but it spent itself most generously on him. It was all around him.

That unflinching realism, that violent contrast of light and dark, those expressive faces, so many of them contorted with hatred, all spoke of Caravaggio. He had been an idol of mine once, as Tintoretto had been. I surrender my idols reluctantly if I surrender them at all, but this painter could stand with them. He had studied the Italians, somewhere and somehow, but he was a German, unmistakably a German.

This painting was the work of a great artist, yet Ludwig said that he was unknown, nobody at all. He was a creator with an original concept, borrowing from no contemporary, a master of chiaroscuro, who handled space and perspective with a sure hand, a portrait painter who had the rare gift of combining individuals into crowds without losing them as individuals. Could it be that to these great gifts there had been added another which destroyed him; the gift of painting so that men, for all time, might find their portraits and, finding them, stand accused?

I looked at the bending coward in the canvas, who would cast his stone in anonymity from behind the crowd, accepting no responsibility for his act. His face was my face and he recalled to me every furtive, cowardly, vile thing that I had ever done. I could not disavow him. A shabby, dirty mediocrity of a man spat upon that patient figure of quiet dignity and his stupid, depraved face repelled me; yet a disciplined, dedicated, intelligent priest had found his face there, and what had it done to him? Could he ever forget it? A tall, finely robed man, fortunate in the gifts of the world, who should be using his gifts to lead men, was reduced to the role of an unreasoning follower of the mob, using the gift of speech that should be reserved for eloquence in mad, hate-inspired cursing. Neil Carlton had seen himself in that figure and collapsed, white-faced, in a chair. We weren't like our prototypes, but how unlike were we?

The door from the corridor opened. Neil was returning and when I sensed that he was not alone, I turned my head. I wanted to rise then, and stop him, but it was too late. Ludwig, too, had risen, protest in his face. Neil had brought Robert to see the painting.

Robert was smiling. He walked slowly, with the closely-spaced steps imposed by his injured spine. There was something too horribly like the scene on the canvas in that slow, careful, trusting approach. He was being led to a cruel experience, one that he would never understand. I did not hear what Neil said to him because he halted before the canvas and his reaction time was swift.

Robert saw all of the details that mattered to him in a few seconds; the scene, the figure of Jesus Christ, and himself. His voice choked in his throat, only a low, guttural sound escaping. For an instant, I thought that he would drop to his knees, but he remembered where he was and who he was. He turned slowly to me and there was both horror and indignation in his eyes.

"Mr. Donner," he said, "it isn't right to do this to me. I wouldn't shake my fist at my Lord and my God."

He had more dignity in shock than any one of us. I had painted his portrait, so his simple, direct mind associated me with what he saw. It was difficult to answer him.

"I didn't paint that picture, Robert," I said. "It was painted three centuries ago."

He believed me because he believed in my friendship, but the bewilderment in his face was awful to witness. There was in it the appeal of the helpless asking help. I had no help to give him. How could I convince him of a reality that my own reason rejected as fantastic and impossible? Ludwig, once more on his feet, and Father Graney turned in his chair, were immobilized as I was. Neil, faced with a responsibility that was his own, accepted it.

"Robert," he said gently, "you have just seen yourself in that painting. I wondered if you would. I found myself there, and Father Graney did, and Mr. Donner, but we could not find one another. There is something miraculous about that picture, something that we do not understand. To my eyes, there is no colored man in the painting. Was there to any of you?"

He half-turned and we answered the question with emphatic negatives. Every face on that canvas was stenciled upon my brain, and not even the accumulated grime since it was cleaned would justify a suspicion that one of the people was a Negro. Robert's face tightened.

"I'm there," he said. "I see myself plain. I am shaking my fist at the Lord. It is something that I would never do."

"Did you ever hear Marian Anderson sing 'Were You There When They Crucified My Lord?'" Neil asked.

"Yes, I did. I have the record of that, a record I play."

Comprehension lighted in Robert's eyes and Neil nodded to that comprehension. "That's how it is," he said. "We were all there, every man who has sinned; swinging the whips, shaking fists, cursing, driving nails. We were all there together, you and I, everyone."

Neil turned Robert away from the painting and walked out with him, still talking in his soft, deep-timbered voice. I had a glimpse then of the kind of shepherd Neil Carlton might have been if he had elected to minister to the few of his own church rather than to the many through a magazine; the weakness of that shepherd and the strength. When he came back, Ludwig was still standing, his hands thrust deep into his pockets.

"I did not like that, Neil," he said. "I do not like it. You should have asked me."

"I know that. I couldn't. You would have refused. It was something that I had to know."

"An intellectual curiosity and unworthy of you."

"No. It was more than intellectual curiosity, worthy or not."

"Robert is the only truly happy person I know. A great person!" Ludwig's voice trembled. "You have destroyed his happiness."

Father Graney roused himself. More than any of us, I believe, he had remained in the state of shock to which the portrait of himself had reduced him. The unanswerable riddle, of course, may have silenced him. Jesuits do not believe in unanswerable riddles and I have never felt that they are fond of miracles.

"Truth is not the enemy of happiness, Ludwig," he said. "Robert is a devout man. He will be all right."

Ludwig did not reply but there was a strange withdrawal in his face, an acceptance of the inevitable which does not imply agreement. He was feeling, perhaps, in some deep chamber of his being that these two men would naturally be allied against him. That, of course, was sensitivity without relation to fact. We were, all four of us, close friends and men become friends as men, not as symbols or exponents. The public humiliation imposed upon us by the painting had sandpapered our nerves and transformed words into little whips but we were still friends.

"Why did Rabbi Marler leave, Ludwig?" I asked. "And why was he angry?"

It was a digressive channel and Ludwig's thought flowed into it, picking up words in its flow without the conscious direction of his mind. He passed his hand over his forehead.

"Rabbi Marler looked at the painting and he would not

listen to me," Ludwig said. "He construed it as anti-Semitic. If he discovered himself, he did not say so. He said that the faces were exaggerated, that the painter had made Jewish caricatures as propaganda to fix upon Jews a responsibility historically untrue. It is a delicate point with him because he believes that historical errors and exaggerations are barriers to brotherhood. He was greatly upset."

I was thinking that there was an interesting point in the fact that Rabbi Marler had not only seen himself in the painting, if he did, but that he had seen all of the faces as different than I, at least, saw them. To me, the faces of the crowd were German, highborn and lowborn. Before I could voice the thought, Neil Carlton asked a question. He was seated once more, with his long legs stretched out, slender fingers curled beneath his chin.

"Ludwig," he asked, "are you in the painting?"

"But, of course. Certainly."

Ludwig seemed startled that there should be any question of the fact. He had his moment of embarrassment, too, as we all stared at him.

"I am that soldier," he said, "that Roman, that big animal pushing back the people."

He could hardly have created a greater sensation. Neil's hands dropped from beneath his chin. Father Graney straightened in his chair, leaning forward, unmasked astonishment in his expression. I do not believe that I moved. I was staring at Ludwig. It was an incongruity of incongruities that Ludwig, out of the four of us, should be a Roman; but that he should be such a Roman!

I tried, mentally, to fit his large head, pale skin, and mild eyes onto that brutal torso and I could not see how it was humanly possible that even he could do it. I remembered his diets in the years that I had known him, the

short-lived, desperate courses of exercise, and I was looking today at the persistent, untidily distributed flesh that
had forever defeated his campaigns against it. What did
the magic inherent in the painting do to his eyes that he
could identify with the steel-hard, perfectly conditioned
body of a professional soldier?

"It is horrible to me," Ludwig said. "If I was defending
him, I could accept the brutality but still say: 'How could
I act so?' I am not defending him. I am smashing people
out of the way so that I can take this man out and kill him.
Just before this, maybe I was flogging him."

The reality of our own experiences was in his every
word because he felt deeply what he expressed and had
been feeling it, no doubt, since he first looked at the
picture. He was a student, a scholar, a lover of beautiful
things, before he was anything else. It was his nature to
shrink from the rough, the brutal, the unfeeling; but he
had been compelled to associate himself with what he ab-
horred, to stand helpless watching himself.

"You, at least, Ludwig, if you identify yourself with
that figure," Father Graney said thoughtfully, "are not acting with malice or hatred, voluntarily doing violence. The
man is a soldier under orders, doing what he believes that
he must."

"To be such a soldier, a man must permit himself to
become a brute."

Neil Carlton sighed. "When we turn men into soldiers,
that is the ideal. And we cannot unmake what we have
made."

We were all looking at the painting again and there was
a different atmosphere in the room. We were four men who
had shared, and were sharing, an experience that no one of
us could accept or believe alone. No one was standing now

while the others remained seated. There were no lines drawn, mentally or in actuality, dividing us. Until Neil asked his question, it had not, incredibly, occurred to me to ask it; nor, apparently, to Father Graney, nor to Neil himself. We had, somehow, accepted Ludwig as the entrepreneur, the master of ceremonies, the producer of a startling and disturbing illusion, loading upon him, subconsciously at least, the guilt and shame we felt at a dramatic reminder that we were ignoble. He was in the painting now with us, sharing the abhorrent association, and we were one.

Ludwig slumped in his chair. "If, from the beginning," he said huskily, "all men could have seen themselves in this moment of history, calling down the blood on *their* children, what a difference it would have made! What a difference in the happiness of people, in civilization, in all things."

"We are not ready to see it yet," Neil said.

"But if people saw this picture? But, no! I know better. It could not be exhibited. It would be the same story as it was before. They would try to burn it."

We were silent and Ludwig could not endure the silence. He turned his head, searching our faces. "How long will it be before it can be done?" he said. "We progress. Would you say fifty years? Can it be, in fifty years, exhibited?"

We met his eyes, but we had no answer for him. We did not know.

Neil Carlton and I walked away from Lorenson's together. We walked four blocks before either of us spoke. "Do you have any ideas about this experience today?" Neil said.

My mind shrugged off all thought of magic and wonder

and the unexplainable. We were surrounded, after all, by people and vehicles and the clattering bang of a big city; by solid realities. A busy city street is not a setting for metaphysics, if there is any reasonable setting for metaphysics.

"We were pretty solemn, Neil," I said. "This is not a religiously minded period of history. That painting could be shown probably without the shocked self-identification drama through which we passed. A lot of today's people would find it amusing. Seeing oneself about to throw a rock at Jesus Christ would not shock everyone as it shocked us. People would go to see it for the novelty of it, for the macabre feature of self-identification."

"No," Neil said. "Nothing would happen for the jokers; nothing at all. I do not pretend to understand that painting but I am certain that beholders would recognize themselves only in such an atmosphere as we created today. Magic, black or white, demands solemnity. A sacramental something. The effect of that picture takes place in the human mind which is mobile. Nothing changes in the painting which is a fixed object; nothing at all."

"It was a great painting, all magic and mumbo-jumbo aside."

"Yes," Neil said. "We will remember the painting. Some of us will think of spiritual matters in connection with it. Eventually we may reach the point of thinking about guilt, about individual and collective guilt. Or we may do a bit of pondering about faith. After all, faith is mysterious, too; more mysterious than hypnotism."

I looked at him then. "Do you believe that illusion of today was the result of hypnotism?"

"No. Do you?"

"No."

We walked a silent block. "I am not going to involve myself in speculation, either," I said. "Guilt and faith are abstractions. None of your theories will be as real as that painting, no matter how tidily you work them and refine them. The painting was as real as we were. We fitted into it because it possessed a reality that we could accept. All else is smoke in the wind."

"Not quite. Nothing has reality without having significance. At Ludwig's that painting was more to you than mere paint on canvas, and it is more to you now."

"Granted. You, however, are trying to find the supernatural in it and I refuse to follow you."

Neil laughed softly. "Kirk," he said, "all of us in that room belonged in one faith or another, all of us excepting you. You are an agnostic, perhaps an atheist, proud in your unbelief. I have an idea, Kirk, that you, of all of us, have the best chance of discovering the meaning in today's experience and that you will discover it."

He laughed again. It was not the laughter of humor; it was that other laughter which eludes definition. "You may even unlock those two greatest of all mysteries, Good and Evil."

He signaled for a taxi with his hand upraised and waved good-bye to me with that same hand as he brought it down. I stood on the crowded sidewalk and watched his taxi move away. I liked Neil Carlton and I admired him but I was not a discoverer of meanings. Life demanded acceptance from me of many things that I did not understand; intricate processes which placed living men on a dead moon, ingeniously designed bombs which could destroy entire cities, many other wonders and seeming miracles. I accepted these things and I did not understand them and I sought no meaning from them; they just were.

CHAPTER TWO

A week after the affair at Ludwig Lorenson's I went to Neil Carlton's home in the late afternoon. Ordinarily I was not on a home-visiting basis with Neil and I had never met his wife. There are strange lines drawn in the lives of friends, lines accepted casually because they make sense. I could not move at Neil's financial level and I was much younger than he was. His social companions, and those of his wife, would be older than I and interested in different things. Art, after all, was only one of Neil's interests and those whom he met in art circles did not belong anywhere else in his life.

We sat in the library, a room of dark wood and regiments of books and a few pictures. The furniture had served through many years and it had accommodated itself to the room. If there had been any clashes in the early years, they had been resolved; everything belonged exactly where it was, not competing for attention with anything else. It was a friendly room, a room in which one could relax, a room with space and without crowding. Our chairs faced each other from opposite sides of the fireplace;

comfortable chairs in which a man could sit without experiencing the sense of sinking.

Neil wore a delicately striped sports jacket of light brown and his necktie was a patterned maroon. His attire never suggested a clergyman but he, himself, often did. He was a solidly built man, not fat. He had a deep tan tint to his skin even in the spring. His head was roughly carved with only a moderately high forehead. He had small pouches under his eyes and the eyes themselves were keenly alert, an odd shade, probably close to what is called hazel. His hair was dark brown and thinning but he still had it. He had a short, casually clipped British-type mustache. His chin was blunt and strong. He was somewhere in his fifties, probably the early fifties.

"I asked you to stop in this afternoon," he said, "because I have been thinking about that picture, unable to get it out of my mind. I have wondered how you have fared with it since your thinking would inevitably take a different shape than mine."

"My thinking has no shape," I said. "I merely walked away from that painting, Neil. We, each of us, saw ourselves in it. That was obviously impossible. Since there was no possible answer, I refused to travel in circles. I have not been thinking about it at all."

"Lucky you! If you can do that, you are most fortunate. Permit me a doubt. *N'importe!* We scraped a surface while we walked on the avenue the other day. Given time, I hoped that you would develop a theory."

"I'll settle for your theory, but only as a subject for dissection, not as fact."

"You would not understand my theory. You would have to have a foundation of faith upon which to set it up. You lack that. You unbelievers are very difficult."

"We listen politely."

"It's not enough. You miss more than you see. No matter now. Do you know anything about the painter of that picture of Ludwig's?"

"Boniface Rohlmann? No. I looked in the books that I have, and I have a few. He was not listed."

Neil nodded. "I had trouble, too. In tough situations I like specialists. I called a librarian whom I know, a very good librarian. I financed two long-distance calls to Europe. My researcher came up with a few things and she swears that we won't get any more."

"I'd be curious."

"Good. Curiosity is the beginning of wisdom."

"And the beginning of other things."

"So I've heard. At any rate, our friend, Rohlmann, was born in Friedheim, Germany, probably in 1619. The Thirty Years' War had just broken out. In the spring of 1632 a Swedish general with the improbable name of Oxenstar occupied Friedheim and the occupation was a brutal one. That fall the Black Plague visited the town. Boniface Rohlmann was thirteen years old in 1632. It must have been difficult for him to learn how to paint, or even think about it."

"Other men did," I said. "The great ones have it inside of them and it comes out. Maybe he thrived—or throve—on adversity."

"Maybe. His work didn't. It may have perished in the war or at the hands of the Church."

"Why the Church?"

Neil smiled. He rose slowly and I knew then that he was holding something back, building to a surprise.

"Sherry, Kirk?" he said.

"Yes, thank you."

He never drank anything stronger than sherry himself and I doubted that he ever served anything stronger to his guests. When he returned with the two glasses I lifted mine to him in salute.

"Lead on," I said. "What follows? Why the Church?"

Neil sipped his sherry and set the glass down precisely. "We have a painter, a very fine painter," he said slowly. "Only two of his paintings are of record now. That one of Ludwig's is not mentioned. Rohlmann had a Madonna in a small church in Würzburg, destroyed by bombs in the war. He had a crucifixion scene in the museum at Dresden. Very little escaped the bombing there. Beyond that, nothing. Rohlmann was not quite forty years old when he died. Why has his work vanished, all trace of him as an artist?"

"It seems impossible," I said. "Why? A man of Rohlmann's obvious command would have an impressive list of work along the way that he came, major work and minor work."

"He didn't. Nothing survives him. Do you know the city of Trier?"

"I haven't been there. I know where it is. It is down near the Luxembourg border."

"Yes. It is probably the oldest city in Germany, perhaps the oldest city in Europe. They have the robe of Christ in the Cathedral, or, at least, one with a strong claim. The only one of the Twelve Apostles buried north of the Alps is there. St. Matthew. They have him in a gold shrine."

"What has this to do with Rohlmann and his painting?"

"I wanted to remind you that Trier is an interesting place." Neil sipped his sherry. He looked at me over the glass with an expression of bland innocence. "You see, that is where Boniface Rohlmann died. He was burned to death at the stake in Trier. As a sorcerer!"

I sat up straight at that. It was a beautifully timed climax of Neil's and a rather astonishing fact. There had been many people burned at the stake in Rohlmann's day, most of them women, and quite a few people were beheaded, but the charge of sorcery was rare and I knew of no painters involved in either witchcraft or sorcery.

Neil was watching me, a barely perceptible smile on his lips. "That is the story," he said, "and perhaps the explanation of the painting in which we all saw ourselves."

"I would find it difficult to accept sorcery as an explanation."

"I know. As I said, unbelievers are difficult. If all the world is physical, purely material, perishable, without an ultimate destiny, nothing in the spiritual world has meaning, nothing in the spiritual world commands faith."

"And if there is no spiritual world?"

"If there isn't you have to ignore Jesus Christ and the eyewitness testimony to miracles, ignore every other religious leader, the vast literature of strange, inexplicable events; events unexplainable in physical terms."

"Or in any other terms."

Neil leaned back, looking toward the ceiling for a few seconds, then brought his eyes back to me.

"Kirk," he said. "Trier is interesting but I don't believe there is a trace left there of Boniface Rohlmann. I'd like you to go to Friedheim where he was born. On assignment. A month. You won't get rich but it should be interesting."

"Thank you," I said, "but to do what?"

"See a Passion Play. Friedheim produces one every ten years, as Oberammergau does, and for the same reason. The people made a vow that they would do it if they were relieved of the plague. They were relieved."

"Interesting, if true. I know about Oberammergau, of course. I never heard of Friedheim."

"A small place. A small play, I imagine. No matter. It has been an unfortunate town in many respects. The important thing is that Boniface Rohlmann was born there and grew up there."

"I still do not understand what I could do in the place."

Neil Carlton straightened slightly. He was holding his wineglass in his left hand. His eyes met mine. "I am not certain that you can do anything. You might absorb something that Rohlmann absorbed in his growing up. Maybe! You could come back and explain that painting of Ludwig's to me. Perhaps!"

I shook my head. "I'm the wrong candidate. You need an ardent believer, someone preconditioned to places like Friedheim and to Passion Plays. I am an agnostic."

"That, if you'll pardon me a comment in passing, is immature of you, but it may be a qualification for this assignment. I would not want from you what I could read in pious books."

"Why not go yourself?"

Neil Carlton sipped his wine, looking at something above and beyond me. I could see the want in him before he spoke. "I would rather go than send you. For many reasons I am not free to go. Will you undertake the assignment for me?"

"Give me twenty-four hours to decide."

Neil set his wineglass down and rose. Our friendly visit was over when he did that. "Twenty-four hours," he said.

"Tomorrow afternoon. The same time. Here!"

I went out to the streets of the city. The city had not changed in the hour that I had spent with Neil Carlton: it was the same old metropolis of snarled traffic and hurry-

ing humans, of noise and odor and crowded space. There
was a mist over it, however, a mist that was not smog.
The city was unreal. I would, I thought, walk onto an airplane and settle back in a comfortable seat; almost immediately, all of this would cease to exist. I would no
longer smell the smells nor see the hurrying people nor
hear the clamorous sounds.

It was a strange mood. The day was a rather grim anniversary and the memory of it had been in my mind all
day, lurking there behind all talk of sorcerer-painters and
magic paintings and Germany in the Middle Ages. One
year ago my ex-wife had died, died violently. She was no
longer linked to me in any way when it happened but I
had experienced shock and all of the usual regrets. The
shock, and the regrets, returned to me on the anniversary
and they brought a mood with them, a somber mood.

I was walking briskly up the avenue. There was a phone
booth and I turned impulsively off course. I called Ludwig
Lorenson and he told me to come right over. He was alone
in his ground-floor office when I entered. I looked for
Robert and did not see him. Ludwig tilted back in his
swivel chair and waved me to a straight chair beside his
desk.

"I can guess why you came," he said. "You want to see
that painting again. Before you ask me, the answer is 'No.'
It must be 'No.'"

"I don't want to see it," I said. "The idea never occurred
to me."

"It occurred to Father Graney. He was here early this
morning. I offended him when I would not again show
him the painting, but I was right." Ludwig made a helpless
shrugging gesture which involved his shoulders and both
of his hands. "I wish that I had never seen that painting. It

was a mistake, showing it. I would not repeat that mistake."

"It had to be shown, Ludwig," I said. "To somebody! You selected the right people. It was too much for them. Not your fault. I am going to Germany because of that painting."

"Why?"

"I want to discover what I can about the painter, about Boniface Rohlmann."

"He was seventeenth century. And obscure. You will discover nothing."

"I will try. He was a great painter, one of the truly great."

"No. He was nobody."

Ludwig said it, and meant it, which told me much about Ludwig. He dealt in established reputations, in the one work out of a painter's many or in a series of works; but he could not look at a work that was isolated, unlinked to any school or to any great reputation and place it where it belonged. That, of course, was not strange. He was knowledgeable in many ways, a man sensitive to beauty, but his eye was the eye of an art dealer, not the eye of a painter.

"Nobody or not, Ludwig," I said, "I am happy that I have met Boniface Rohlmann, if only in one painting. He was interesting, a mystery. I know how he died."

Ludwig's eyes narrowed. All of his features were still. It was obvious then that he was not as ignorant of Rohlmann as he was willing to pretend. He was waiting for me to finish my statement, to fill in the details of which I had claimed knowledge.

"He was burned to death in Trier," I said, "in 1661. As a sorcerer."

Ludwig released his held breath in a soft sigh. "Trier?"

he said. "I think not. But have it as you please. What else
do you know?"

"That he was born in Friedheim in 1619."

"Nothing else?"

"That's right."

"And on that you are going to Germany."

"It is a beginning and an end. I'll find something in
between."

"You will find not much." Ludwig played with a ball-
point pen that he took from the top of his desk and turned
around between his fingers. "This Rohlmann had something wrong with him. Not sorcery. I do not believe in
that. He did not stay long in any place. He did not belong
anywhere. A seventeenth-century hippie!"

"No. He was a worker, a hard worker. He had to be."

"On one painting you cannot tell."

"Yes. I can."

"You are young. Young people know everything. Maybe
you are right. He painted that one that I showed you in
Bamberg."

"Bamberg! I've been there. How do you know?"

Ludwig looked at something off to my left, not seeing
me at all. "I do not know," he said. "I was told and I
believe. The painting came to me from Würzburg. In the
Nazi time it was buried three basements down with many
other things. The Nazis did not find it and the bombs did
not go down so far when the Americans and the British
bombed the city. It has taken many years for the heirs of
the owners to establish claim to the property. A complicated business, law; it can never be simple."

"If I went there, to Würzburg, could I meet the people
who sent you that painting, talk with them?"

"No. I would not reveal their names. They know nothing of painting or painters. They could tell you nothing. You would alarm them. They are entitled to their privacy."

"I wouldn't disturb their privacy. Somebody preserved that painting from harm. Somebody knew what he was doing. They looked at the painting, these people in Würzburg. They must have seen what we saw. They would know more about the painting than we know."

Ludwig shook his head. "They know nothing, nothing of art." He made a weary gesture with one hand. "My people respect art, paintings, books, things of beauty, things of great skill. They respect them. They try to preserve them. They do not necessarily understand them. Believe me on it! I will not supply you with names in Würzburg. I have sound reasons."

"I respect your reasons, Ludwig," I said, "but tell me one more thing. The other night you said that the painting caused trouble when it was shown. Where? You said that people tried to burn it. When?"

"Gossip. Rumors. Very old gossip. Very old rumors. I should not repeat such things."

"I would like to know."

"There is nothing. People invent things. People exaggerate. Such things are of no value." Ludwig rose and I rose with him. I knew that our visit was over. He walked to the door of his office with me.

"You will discover nothing about this artist, Rohlmann," he said, "but have lunch with me when you return. I will hear about your trip."

I smiled at that. I would discover nothing but he wanted to be certain that he would share that nothing. "Certainly, Ludwig," I said. "We will do that."

I remembered something then that I should have remembered earlier. "I did not see Robert when I came in. Is he all right?"

"No." Ludwig's mouth tightened. "He is very ill. He should never have seen that painting. He was a happy man. Neil Carlton betrayed the trust that I placed in him. He is no longer my friend."

"He *is* your friend, Ludwig. He had to know if a black man would find himself in that painting. Or he believed that he had to know."

Ludwig shook his head slightly. "I hope that you have a good trip. Be sure to see me when you return."

We shook hands and then I was back on the street again, back to the noise and the odor and the unreality of it. In its way, the environment, too, was a portrait by a sorcerer. It disappeared when one left it but one was moved by it, affected by it, in perhaps a thousand ways while one remained within the realm of its influence.

All of which seemed to indicate that I had lost my slender grip on common sense. I probably needed to get away, to go somewhere, anywhere.

CHAPTER THREE

Friedheim was not on the railroad line, nor on the auto-bahn. Two buses a day made the journey to Friedheim from Munich. The bus station for that particular line was on an obscure back street. I had lived for two months in Munich at one time but I had never seen that street, nor the bus station. A stout man behind a short counter sold me a ticket cheerfully. A series of posters on the wall behind him urged the beholder to visit various towns with quaint and unfamiliar names. A half-dozen people sat, waiting, on long benches. I did not know if they were waiting to go to Friedheim and I did not care. I did not feel sociable. The man behind the counter told me that my bus would be number 11. There was a blackboard with chalked schedules on the wall behind the long benches. It informed me that bus 11 would leave in fifteen minutes. I knew that, being German, it would not leave in fourteen minutes, or in sixteen, but exactly and precisely in fifteen.

There were three buses in line outside the bus station and 11 was in the forward, lead position. It was an old bus, quite obviously old, but it was not shabby. The bloom of youth had left it but it was clean. The door was open but there was no one inside, neither passengers nor crew. I was carrying only one bag, a fairly large one. I put it in a clear section at the back of the bus and took the front seat across the aisle from the driver, a seat providing vision through a side window and through the driver's window. I was set for a journey and I did not mind waiting.

The girl arrived in less than five minutes. She had a husky youth carrying her bags. There were two large bags and a small one. She was carrying a medium-sized black handbag and a blue Pan American flight bag. She stood hesitantly outside the bus door and looked in doubtfully. She looked at me then and was not reassured.

"Is this the bus to Friedheim?" she asked.

She spoke in German so I answered her in German: "That is what they told me."

She seemed dissatisfied. I had an idea that she had not seen me, that she was aware of me as a presence in the bus, no more than that.

"It is strange," she said, "that there is no driver. The bus is supposed to leave in six minutes."

"Eight minutes."

She looked at me then. She was a slender girl and her hair was the first feature that one noticed. It flowed out from under her floppy gray felt hat and, without getting too color-technical about it, it was auburn. She had dark eyes and a straight nose and a full-lipped mouth, not sensual but well defined. Her cheekbones pressed gently under her skin and her chin was firm without protruding.

"This is the bus that goes to Friedheim," said the husky youth with the bags.

She stepped aside and let him put the bags in the back of the bus with mine. She was, obviously, still unhappy about a bus without a driver, a bus that did not measure up in appearance to the bus she had anticipated.

"I have the best seat in this vehicle," I said, "and if you will share it, you may have the window."

I spoke in English and that startled her. She turned her head and she was looking in my direction but not actually seeing me. "You're American!"

"How did you guess?"

"I didn't know. Everyone has been speaking German. You should have told me sooner."

"I couldn't. It belonged later in the conversation where I put it."

She snapped her fingers. "Of course. We weren't having a conversation, were we? No, thank you. I will sit across the aisle."

"Fine," I said. "That whole side of the bus is yours."

She was still worrying about the missing driver and when she took her across-the-aisle seat, she perched on it rather than settling comfortably in. This was probably normal. The nervousness of women seems to express itself most easily in irrelevancy. She might not actually care whether the bus had a driver or not; she was unsure of herself and she needed some way of expressing that insecurity. I shrugged her off and looked out of my window. I did not worry about her or about the bus. The driver arrived with three minutes to spare and before he had time to ask for her ticket, she asked him if the bus went to Friedheim.

"*Ja,*" he said and, out of compulsion or politeness, he rattled off the names of nine other towns at which it stopped. He took the tickets then and two men in shabby clothes, obviously regular passengers, boarded the bus and exchanged greetings with him. We started precisely on time.

Our route took us through an uninspired section of Munich. The girl fidgeted. I could recognize the fidgeting without looking at her.

"Is that offer of your window seat still open?" she asked meekly.

"Open until we pass the city limits."

"I'll take it."

She followed her words across the aisle and I surrendered the window seat to her. She could look forward through the windscreen instead of staring at the driver's back or she could look out of the window on her right, or she could look at me. She looked at me.

"I am afraid that I was not very polite when you spoke to me," she said.

"Not notably."

"I'm sorry. I was disturbed. I'm usually polite."

"I am certain of it."

We were two strangers in a foreign country with no clues to background, occupations or reasons for being; two people making meaningless conversation as a prelude to some relationship unguessable. We would be fellow passengers, probably no more than that, but one needed an awkward warmup to even qualify as fellow passengers.

"I am Joan Terrill," she said.

She hesitated, then decided not to mention her mission in Friedheim, whatever it might be. I was only mildly curious.

"I am Kirk Donner," I said, "and I am representing, temporarily, two art magazines and a powerful Protestant publishing house: powerful, that is, as such things go."

"Oh."

She looked out the window and there wasn't much at which to look. I knew then, without her telling me, that

she had some kind of a journalistic mission taking her to
Friedheim. She was disconcerted at the prospect of competition.

"There will be quite a few journalists, correspondents
and photographers," I said. "A Passion Play only happens
every ten years."

"Yes."

Her eyes came back to me, then went away again. She
was a pretty girl, not poster pretty but natural, smooth-
skinned, clean; a touch of make-up, not much, and no blue
around her eyes.

"I wonder why there aren't more people on this bus,"
she said. "I thought that because of the Passion Play the
bus would be crowded."

"Too soon. It doesn't start for a week. The cast are all
Friedheim people. So, I imagine, are the technicians. They
live there."

"Did you ever see a Passion Play? Here, or—" She hesitated, looked at me from the corners of her eyes and decided that, ten years ago I had not. "That is, in Oberammergau?"

"No. I'm not too interested now."

She straightened. "Why not?"

"Because I do not believe that any plague ever stopped
because people promised to do plays. I do not believe that
people go on with plays because of vows. In Oberammergau, I imagine, the thing grew big and they couldn't stop.
The play was the town industry, the factory, the way of
life, the money. Friedheim is smaller but the principle is
the same. The play is a habit and they can't drop it."

The girl was staring at me, wide-eyed, and I had a
moment of regret. She was one of the believers and I had
trampled all over her. It had not been necessary to do that.

She was sitting in her seat and I in mine. We could relax as easily in our own beliefs and convictions, as we did in the bus seats, not interested in converting each other; merely two different people in two different seats.

"Prejudice is the most immature thing in the world," Joan Terrill said. "It cannot even read history. It knows all the wrong answers to every question. I think your ideas about Friedheim and Oberammergau are absurd."

She turned away then and stared out of the window. If I own a wry smile I probably used it. I had been regretting my roughness. My life should have taught me that women are not helpless. Obviously, it had not. A man has to keep on learning such lessons as that, over and over again.

We were out of town now and rolling through the springtime; orchards in bloom, the blossoms standing out clearly as small pictures then vanishing in a long panorama of white and pink. We rumbled into our first town, a place of quaint old-fashioned houses and cobbled streets. It was a quick stop, then out again to the open springtime.

"The country is incredibly beautiful," the girl said.

She forgave me for being me in the uttering of that remark, so I forgave her, too. "You've never been in Germany before?" I asked.

"Never."

"You speak German well."

"I studied it. High school and college. I was always pretty good at the things I studied."

"I can believe it."

She was, I thought, one of the earnest souls. She would be good at anything and everything if anything and everything interested her, or compelled her or commanded her with the voice of righteousness. Most earnest souls look like stolid characters, like grim strivers and conscientious doers of deeds. This girl did not resemble such creatures at all in appearance. She looked like a potentially challenging date, but as a conversationalist she was heavy going.

"I was surprised," she said, "when I learned that Friedheim is a town where they make violins, and cellos and guitars. That is all they do there outside of the Passion Play."

"Not precisely. They sell things to one another, I imagine, and there will be a few plumbers around and carpenters and an automobile mechanic or two."

"Of course," she said impatiently. "All towns have those. But, the main activity, the center—"

She broke off because we were rolling through a particularly beautiful stretch of country. There was a wide meadow with the pink of wild crab-apple trees bordering it. In the near distance there was a church, one of the onion-steeple churches that Americans associate with Russia but which are more accurately associated with Germany; if for no other reason than that Germany has so many more churches than Russia. Beyond the church there was water, incredibly blue water, one of the numerous lakes.

"There are so many surprises," the girl said.

The statement did not tie to anything that she had said previously but she was staring out of the window, paying no attention to me, and I understood what she meant. I understood, too, her vaguely made point about the "center of things." One felt that center in Germany. Mittenwald was another violin town and Oberammergau shipped its wood carvings all over the world and there was a town in the Black Forest where practically everyone painted on glass. Ströbeck produced chess pieces. One discovered such facts and one was interested or one was not. I was not certain that this girl would be interested.

The view of the mountains broke upon us without warning. We followed a descending curve into a valley and there were low hills on our right, snowclad, towering peaks behind them.

Joan Terrill drew her breath in sharply but she made no comment. I, too, was silent. Any comment would have been inadequate. This was a view for the gods; fruit trees in blossom, vineyards green on the hills and beyond that the snow.

We rolled through a town and stopped at two. Each town, no matter how small, was distinctively itself. There was the inevitable church, sometimes two churches, old-fashioned houses with steeply slanted roofs, fountains in squares, images of town patron saints, crucifixes. Our two fellow passengers left us and we did not pick up any more.

The feeling that, apart from the driver, we were the only travelers made me more sharply aware of the girl beside me. She seemed to feel something of what I was feeling. She turned her head, momentarily, away from the window.

"You said, I believe, that you are on an assignment for a Protestant magazine. Of what faith are you?"

It was merely an attempt at conversation on a more personal basis than scenery and I should have met it for what it was. A person who thought in terms of faiths or religions would ask a question like that. I wasn't content with it; I had to proclaim myself.

"If you mean religion, I haven't any. I'm working for a magazine. The fact that it is Protestant is only incidental."

"I see."

She turned again to the window and I had a sense of

dropped curtain. She had tuned me out and I would have felt slightly ridiculous in trying to pick up the conversation again at the low point in which we had left it. The scenery flowed past and the bus rocked slightly on the uneven road. The girl looked out at the trees and the fields and the mountains. We were approaching Friedheim when she turned.

"I should have told you sooner," she said. "I am on assignment, too. I am, or I was, a research worker for *Sphere*. They sent me over here to write the story of the Passion Play."

"You are lucky. One cannot do better for a sponsor than *Sphere*."

"I thought so. At any rate, I will be working here. I am not just a tourist."

She turned back to her window and I was not certain that her deflation of me had been deliberate. It could have been. She disapproved of me and we were at opposite poles of feeling and belief. *Sphere* was one of the great magazines of the world. I knew a few of the minor editors and I had been in the *Sphere* offices several times. It was difficult to fit this girl into the picture. The young men of *Sphere* were cynical moderns, less interested in an event or a novel or a work of art than they were in the wise-guy phrase that would destroy it.

"How did they ever send a girl like this one overseas on a story?" I thought.

Almost immediately the answer came. It was obvious, inevitable. She was perfect for it. None of the bright boys could look at a Passion Play without wearing a superior smile, nor at a place like Friedheim without digging into the comedy barrel. This girl was a square and she would play the whole sequence straight. Even if she exaggerated,

as she probably would, her story would be in the spirit of
the Passion Play idea, in tune with it. Nobody would read
a story about a Passion Play who did not want to be in
tune with it.

The valley had narrowed and one could no longer see
the back range of mountains. We had low hills on either
side of us. The road curved downward and the town was
on our right. The driver did not take the direct route in. He
swung behind the main street and entered the town by a
narrow road. There was a paved courtyard and a stone
bus station which looked older than the age of motor
buses.

"Friedheim," the driver called.

Two elderly men came aboard to pick up our luggage.
The girl indicated which were hers and named her hotel,
Die Geiger. Her finger lingered over each bag in turn until
the bag was picked up. "Do I need a cab?"

"No. You follow me. It is very short."

She would have followed him, ignoring me, but I would
not have that, little as it mattered. "It was a good trip," I
said. "I enjoyed traveling with you. I'll see you around
town."

"Oh!" Her eyes widened slightly. "I thought, of course,
that we would be at the same hotel. I did not think, I
guess; I just assumed that there was only one hotel."

"There are two. I am at the Bahnhof."

"I'll see you then, as you say, around town." She smiled
faintly. "It was a pleasant trip for me, too."

She followed her man who put the bags on a two-wheel
pushcart and moved slowly across the courtyard. My man
took my bag in the opposite direction and I asked no questions. I knew that hers would be the best hotel and that
mine would be what was left. It didn't matter. I was draw-

ing clear air into my lungs and there was a silvery twilight
and the air was chill. The adventure on which I had em-
barked was suddenly quite real.

We walked three blocks. The houses that I saw were
whitewashed and brightened with splashily painted biblical scenes. The Bahnhof was half-timbered, steep-roofed
as all the houses were, and tall. One did not have any idea
how large it was until he walked down one of the corridors
inside. My room was on the second floor, with bath and
toilet down the hall. It was a simple room with a bed, a
dresser, a bedside table and one chair. There were two
small prints on the walls; Caravaggio's *Supper at Emmaus*
and Melozzo da Forli's *Angel with a Violin*. I was grateful
that they had not overwhelmed me with religious art.

The town of Friedheim was just outside but I felt no
urgency about it. It would be there tomorrow and the next
day, and the next. It was early yet for supper so I decided
to dedicate this island in time to Neil Carlton. The bedside
table was as solid as a granite boulder, so I used that as a
desk.

Dear Neil: (I wrote)

This is where the story starts if there is a story. I visited
Würzburg and Bamberg first and I spent enough time in
each of them to convince myself that I would not find Boniface Rohlmann there, nor any trace of him. I talked to town
clerks and librarians and people in the museums. They have
people at intervals seeking information about Rohlmann but
they could not tell me what inspires people to inquire about
him. Where do they discover his name, or anything that
stimulates them to seek for more?

One painting of his hung in a Würzburg church which was
almost totally destroyed in the bombing. It was a Madonna

in a town that seems never to have lacked Madonnas. Nobody whom I found remembered it and there is absolutely no available record of Rohlmann living in Würzburg or working there. In Bamberg, oddly enough, there was a simple museum entry on a card which listed the Würzburg Madonna of B. Rohlmann with the one added note: circa 1651. If that date is correct, he painted the Madonna ten years before his death. I wish that I could have seen it but it is gone with the ash and the rubble.

I rode in the bus from Munich with a girl from *Sphere,* assigned to this Passion Play. She is a nice girl who will believe everything she sees and half of what she's told—and who will write with the passion of utter belief in whatever already occupies her brain, never questioning how it got there. Interesting, isn't it, that *Sphere* is taking note of this obscure place.

Incidentally, this is a violin-making town; violins, violas, cellos, guitars plus bows and other hardware. There is an open court in front of the hotel and a fountain with three string-instrument children in bronze. It is pretty good, not as old as it tries to pretend but pretty good.

I hear the dinner bell, I hope. More anon.

　　　　　　　　　　　　　　　　　　　　　　Kirk.

CHAPTER FOUR

Freidheim in the morning was an operetta without music. The bright sunlight flowed across an incredibly blue sky and dropped down on green hills and on white houses with sloping red roofs. The doors of the houses were painted in all the colors and all of the hues. The people who walked the streets belonged in them; men in Alpine costumes or dark trousers with red or green jackets, women in long wide skirts of blue, brown, yellow, or green. The men wore beards, with a few exceptions, neatly trimmed beards that suggested the apostles or the prophets. The town was not Nazareth or Jerusalem, of course, but to a painter's eye it could suggest either. After all, we always did paint the people and the places we knew, no matter what myth or legend we portrayed.

I walked past Die Gieger but I did not see Joan Terrill. There was a truly old fountain with a figure in bronze that had weathered the centuries. A date in the base read 1667. It was a simple figure of an old man holding a violin. He was not playing it, merely holding it, holding it reverently. The effect was most impressive.

There was a fountain before the Town Hall, too, with a

saint figure, male, in a cassock. The Town Hall was my first objective, a small picturesque building in which the business of the municipality was conducted.

There was a matronly woman at a desk behind a counter in a large room off the entrance hall. She had dark hair and mild blue eyes and a pleasant expression. Her face was broad and full. She gave the impression of solid maternity rather than of fat. She left her desk and met me at the counter, inquiry in her eyes.

"I am seeking information about a painter," I said. "He was born here. His name was Boniface Rohlmann."

There was a flicker of recognition in her eyes when I mentioned the Rohlmann name but she shook her head. "I do only routine things," she said. "You will have to speak to my husband."

"Where is he?"

"He is rehearsing. You could not see him now. He is in the play."

"When could I see him?"

She looked at me thoughtfully and something about me must have reassured her. "He will stop at the Eisenhut at five before he comes home to dinner. If you drink a beer with him he might be more informative."

She smiled broadly then and I liked her. "I'll do that," I said. "But I do not know his name."

"A simple name. Josef Paskert."

"Josef Paskert. I will remember. What part does he have in the play?"

Her smile disappeared. As I was to discover, everything touching on the Passion Play was a serious matter, with no levity tolerated.

"He is Judas Iscariot." There was a defensive note in her voice and I could understand that. A man might easily be associated with the part he played and a wife, of course, would share the association. "It is a splendid role," she said, "second only to Jesus in the play."

"It must be; and difficult to play."

"Yes." Her eyes warmed to me for that bit of understanding. "My husband, Josef, is a very fine actor. It is unbelievable. It is, perhaps, because his life is not exciting. He does not carve wood or make fine instruments. Only this!"

She indicated the office with a swift spreading of her hands. "God has given him a great gift, perhaps, because he has need of it."

This was the deeply religious soul speaking and it had its own eloquence. She did not realize how moving she was in that small scene. She was not seeing herself at all, or thinking about herself. She was thinking about her husband. She wanted others who met her husband to see in him the something that she saw, to understand in him what she understood. I would have liked to paint her as she appeared in that arrested moment.

"That is an interesting thought," I said. "I shall enjoy meeting your husband."

I went out to the streets of the town again: the bearded men and the quaintly costumed women. No town in the Holy Land had ever looked like this, none of the people of the Bible stories had worn clothing such as these, nor faces such as these; but the effect, the total effect, was oddly biblical. One moved back through the centuries on the streets of Friedheim.

Judas would not be available for a beer until evening and I did not feel like talking to anyone else. Sightseeing did not appeal at the moment, either, nor research. I took my folding easel up a rather steep little hill and sat contemplating the town, equipped to sketch it if the mood was right, satisfied to merely look at it if no creative drive developed.

The town at first was a pattern of steeply slanted roofs, red for the most part but with the pattern broken occasionally by a roof of gray or yellow. The church with its onion-shaped steeple stood on rising ground which gave it a commanding position. Beyond the church and the roofs there was a curving river. The streets curved, too, and made weird geometric patterns.

It did not do to be carried away and credit an artistic sense, or taste, to the design of those streets. The design came down from the Middle Ages and so did many of the streets. A straight street would have been murder to the defenders of a town like this in the centuries of pikes and swords and cavalry. A curving street, with sharp corners to turn, made trouble for an attacker if defenders waited around the turn. So much for origins. Now the effect was art, pure art.

Friedheim, although smaller then, must have looked much as it did now when the Swedish general, Oxenstar, rode down on it a long time ago. The Germans, particularly in the small towns, have a tendency to rebuild in kind when a building is destroyed, to expand in kind when expansion is the order of the day. The character of a town is preserved in that way although the years roll over it.

I looked down lazily on Friedheim, content to look at it. It took me a long period of looking to discover that the town was shaped like a star, a five-pointed star. Once I saw the star I could not escape it. It was there, unmistakably, the shape of the town. I could not believe that the town had been planned that way, nor consciously shaped. On ground level one would lose all sense of the star. It had to be observed from where I sat, or from a comparable level, and rural towns are not planned or built by dreamers on heights; they come into being under the hands of workers compelled by the necessities of moments, practical people who do not look to the future in terms of developing shapes. There was no sane, practical reason for Friedheim to be shaped like a star, so one could not believe that anyone had ever planned it thus; it merely happened.

I set up my easel and prepared to sketch the streets and the rooftops, the church and the river. My eyes were filled with them and then I heard the tinkling of a bell. I had been aware of bells, gentle bells, on the hillside, without accepting them as an intrusion. This single bell intruded, imperative rather than gentle. I looked into the eyes of the ugliest cow that I had ever seen.

All of the other animals were up the hill, placidly grazing and paying no attention to the companions of their day or the world in which they lived. The cow which had joined my world had a wondering look. It would have been easy to credit it with the mental agony claimed by so many of today's young; the who-am-I, where-am-I, why-am-I-here kick. It seemed to have no purpose in coming within my range unless it was to look at me, or have me look at it. It was an animal of dirty brown color, a white face that was dotted with black spots irregularly spaced, heavy black circles around both of its eyes. The bell hanging from a cord around its neck had a design of rosettes stamped in the metal, and, incongruously, a crucifix. We gazed at each other, the creature and I. I was the one who capitulated.

"Okay," I said, "I'll sketch your portrait."

The cow never moved. It held its pose beautifully and,

in spite of its ugly features, it managed a pleasant expression. There was a lot of ham in that animal. There was a period of my life that had made me an authority on ham and hamming. My wife had been an actress and I had been exposed to a lot of it.

Sketching that cow was fun, a task without a purpose, work to no reasonable end. I gave it the best that I had and, perversely, I liked what I achieved. I had no regrets for the star-shaped town on which I had not started. When I rose to put the sketch back in the protector, the cow broke pose and moved six or eight feet away. She stood there watching me and I waved to her before I started back to the town.

"Thank you, Milky," I said. "I had a good time."

The town, with its variety of blossoms, its sill-pots filled with geraniums, its other-century dresses and its apostolic beards was real again; not a star-shaped abstraction viewed from a hill. Joan Terrill was swinging down the street from the church, breathless vitality in a gray-blue suit. She saw me and waved.

"What did you find in your day?" she asked cheerfully.

"Nothing much. A cow that I couldn't resist sketching."

Her forehead wrinkled in a semi-frown. "I had no right to ask," she said. "I don't mind telling you what I found." She counted her items off on the fingers of her left hand.

"A marvelous old church. It doesn't seem real. And the inevitable cemetery. And a fascinating museum. I found headquarters of the play and registered as a correspondent. I have an appointment with the man who plays Jesus, but not until after a performance of the play. He won't see anybody before the play." She drew a deep breath. "Best of all, I have someone to answer all my questions,

the handsomest man I have ever seen, the man who acts
the role of John in the play."

She had had a full day, which only emphasized my
own laziness, my failure to come to grips. "You don't
believe that I sketched a cow?" I said.

"Of course not. But that is all right. I have no right
to know what you did."

I took the sketch out of the protector and showed it
to her. Her eyes widened. "That is good. Awfully good.
Almost breathing. But why in the world?"

"I asked myself that same question. I didn't come up
with an answer."

She shook her head, obviously conceding me. "John's
name is really Johann Veit. I have to meet him now at
the hotel, in a few minutes."

The temptation was strong to tell her about my own
date, to say casually that I was about to share a beer
with Judas Iscariot; but the idea seemed a bit competitive.
I said good-bye to her and walked up the hill in the
direction from which she had come. I passed the church
without any impulse to enter it. The way was downhill
again once I had passed it and there was a crisscross-
ing network of streets. The Eisenhut was off the direct
route, a low stone building behind a stone wall. Above
the door in the fence there was a cast-iron sign with a
metal wineglass within an iron wreath and with the name
EISENHUT below it. There were clusters of fresh grape
stems twined in the cast-iron design, serving notice that
the new wine was available. Inside there was a long, cool
room of many tables, a dimly lighted room. A short, heavy
man approached me when I entered.

"I hope to meet Mr. Paskert here," I said.

He nodded. "I could serve you a drink."

"I'll wait until he comes."

"Be at home."

He went back to the three men with whom he had been visiting. I sat at a small table halfway down the room. Several men entered after I did, all except one with beards. I dismissed them, one by one, with a glance, but I knew my man when he came, without a momentary doubt.

This man had to be Judas. He looked tall but actually he was no taller than I; five foot ten. He was broad and blocky and he carried himself like a soldier. He was in his early forties; maybe the late thirties. He had a full beard, nicely shaped. His hair was dark, his beard much lighter. He was wearing a tan shirt and green trousers and oxfords which had seen much wear. The tavern-keeper spoke to him and he looked toward my table. I rose in my place and the man crossed the room to me.

"My friend, Bruno, says that you have asked for me."

"You are Mr. Paskert, Josef Paskert?"

He shook his head. "Judas. While the play runs I am called nothing else. What can I do for you?"

"I would like to buy you a drink and I would like to ask you questions."

"The drink is acceptable. You spare me from paying for it. The questions are another matter. I may not answer them."

"Suit yourself on that."

He seated himself at the table and that was a signal which registered immediately. A young man appeared magically, bearing two tall steins of beer on a tray. Judas said, "Ahhh!" and took a deep swallow.

"The questions," he said.

"What do you know of Boniface Rohlmann?"

His eyes were momentarily intent, then they retreated. "Little. Why do you concern yourself?"

"I saw a painting of his in New York. It is not listed in any of the places I have searched. I understand that he was born here."

"I have never seen a painting of his. What was it like, this painting?"

"It was very fine. It was a painting of Christ in the courtyard under Pilate's balcony. He had been condemned to death and the soldiers were leading him away, probably to nail him on the cross, or to make him carry it. The mob had stopped them and they were shouting at Jesus."

Judas nodded. "I know the scene. You say that the painting is well done?"

"Very well done. My feeling was that the painter could stand proudly with the best of the Italians. Who was he?"

"I don't know. People come here to inquire. I am the town clerk when I am not in the play. I cannot help them."

"Where do they hear of him in the first place, these people who inquire?"

"That I do not know. When I inquire, they are reticent." Judas looked at the bottom of his empty stein and I signaled to the boy to bring two more. "Thank you," Judas said, "I am faster than you at drinking beer, more adept. You have heard how he died, this Rohlmann?"

"I was told that he was burned to death as a sorcerer in 1661. Is that correct?"

"I, too, have heard that. I do not know. It was a bad time for sorcerers and witches, the seventeenth century; and the sixteenth. It may be that they belong to secret societies, these people who inquire. Secret societies may keep records of sorcerers, of many things."

"Do you believe in secret societies?" I asked.

"Of a certainty. One knows that they exist. There is no question."

"And witches? And sorcerers?"

Judas drank deeply of his beer. "The tone of your voice tells me," he said, "that you do not accept these things. You are far away from them, so they do not exist. You are mistaken. Do you have another question?"

"Yes. About Rohlmanns. Do any of them still live in Friedheim and what do the town records reveal about them?"

"There are none here now. Nor in towns close to this one. I have been asked that question before. There are no Rohlmanns in the Munich phone book but there are three Rollmans. Four Rohlmanns paid taxes in Friedheim until 1728. After that, none. The last Rohlmann of record here was a woman, Elizabeth. She was buried in 1742. Sixty-seven years old, with no kin of record. They were not an outstanding family. There is no record of a painter."

He looked at me inquiringly, inviting another question, knowing in his own mind what the question should be, as I knew in mine. I took my time, letting him wait.

"Where did they live, these Rohlmanns? In what part of town?"

The question pleased him. "The old part," he said. "Oxenstar's officers took many houses and lived in them. In 1632. The rest of the houses were looted, damaged, burned. Oxenstar himself was here only a week. The street where he lived is called Schwedischstrasse. The best houses were there. There is also Friedlichstrasse and Gebetstrasse, equally old. Also the Hanswurst Kreis."

"And the last Rohlmann, Elizabeth? Where did she live?"

Judas rose. "She is in the churchyard." He smiled. "It is the only address I have."

"The plague was 1632?"

"It was. First the Swedes, then the plague, then the vow. A year of events." He smiled again, a burly genial man whom it was impossible to accept as Judas. "I must go to my dinner," he said. "Think of more questions and we shall meet again."

"I will do that," I said.

There were a number of beer drinkers in the place now. They all greeted Judas as he moved toward the door. He was an interesting man. Knowing him was, at least, partial recompense for the time that I had wasted in sketching a cow. The girl wonder from *Sphere* was far ahead of me on research at the end of the first day. I would have to go to work.

Tonight, I decided suddenly, I would dine at her hotel instead of my own. It would be interesting to see what the competition offered.

CHAPTER FIVE

The Geiger was a much newer hotel than the Bahnhof but it was, unmistakably, a rural hotel: spotless and shining but with utility dominating even the appearance of the place. The dining room was large, disproportionately large if one ignored the fact that people came to Friedheim for the play, with a need for meals but no need for overnight accommodation. It was a plain octagonal room with tables laid in a precise pattern. The walls were decorated with murals of the Passion Play and against the west wall there were booths, small caves under pseudo-stone arches with tables that would serve four people or, more happily, two.

Joan Terrill was in the middle booth with a blond young man. She had described him as "the handsomest man I have ever seen" and she could have been right. He was beardless and his profile was sharply cut; clean lines in outline and bronzed skin inside the lines. He had full curly hair which he wore long. I was weary of that fashion in the United States but in Friedheim they were trying to re-create the zero century. This man was the John of the Passion Play, the "beloved disciple" of Christ.

The couple in the booth did not see me and I could not stare at them; so, after the first photographic impression registered, I dismissed them from my mind. I had veal to think about, veal cooked as only Germans cook it, vegetables that had never been canned or frozen, and white wine of the country. I did not think about Joan Terrill and her escort again until they stopped at my table on their way out.

"Mr. Donner," she said, "this is Mr. Johann Veit who plays the Apostle John in the play."

She was wearing a coppery dress which emphasized the copper in her hair and she had obviously been having a good time. I had commanded no such animation from her on the bus. The apostle was only slightly taller than she was, a slender young man in a brown jacket, yellow shirt and dark slacks. He lifted his eyes to mine and I was not prepared for him.

Looking into his eyes was like looking into the eyes of a girl.

These were eyes of soft and gentle blue, but there was an odd effect of other eyes behind the eyes one saw. His voice was medium tenor, a pleasant voice without any falsetto in it.

"We were talking about you during dinner, Mr. Donner," he said.

"I told him that you are painting the portrait of a cow."

Joan Terrill smiled at me and the apostle laughed softly. "I have a good model," I said. "She does not talk much."

They left me and I finished my supper. When I walked out again there was a pale twilight and the lights in houses were shielded by veils of mist. There was a perfume in the air that was a blend of many flowers and many blossoms. Sounds blended, too; string instruments in houses

or gardens. There were few people on the streets and no
autos. It was two blocks to Bretestrasse which one could
translate loosely as Broadway. There was more light, a
few more people, but nothing that could be called night
life. I was restless but there was nothing in Friedheim,
nothing for me, to provide an outlet for restlessness. I
walked back to the hotel and my room.

John still disturbed me, so I put him out of my mind.
He was not a responsibility of mine and tomorrow was
going to be a big day. I did not have to catch up with
the busy correspondent of the *Sphere* but I had to do a
little work for Neil Carlton and his Protestant magazine.
If I uncovered anything about Boniface Rohlmann, that
would be a bonus. I was filled with firm resolves and
they moved in me rhythmically, harmoniously. They put
me to sleep almost instantly.

The morning was another matter. I did not want to
do anything. It took the stern exercise of mental whips
to drive me to the office of the Passion Play, a three-room
affair in a large flat-roofed building. A girl behind a desk
referred me to a man behind another desk. The man's
name was Rudolf Lobinger. He had a beard but it did
not look apostolic: it was too neat, too sleekly contoured.

"Oh, yes," he said, when I presented my press passes.
"Mr. Carlton wrote to advise us that you were coming.
There is another American correspondent, a Miss Terrill.
Did you know that?"

I told him that I knew it and he seemed to consider
that quite intelligent of me. He explained patiently that
out of regard for foreign correspondents and their community of interests, he had reserved for me a seat beside
Miss Terrill at the Press showing of the Passion Play, the

very first performance. He had also arranged for us to interview the man who played Christ in a joint interview.

"He limits interviews," he said, "and will give none until after the first performance." He beamed at me, practically taking a bow. "I hope that my effort pleases you."

"It delights me," I told him. "Does Miss Terrill know that we are doing all these things together?"

"No, no. It will surprise her. I have not seen her since I arranged your tickets. She has already her tickets."

"She will be very happy," I said.

The thought of how happy she would not be was a brightener for my day. Suddenly I had work to do and the desire to do it. I walked a few blocks to the museum. It was a good place to start. In any town or city a museum provides an introduction. Most of what one finds in a museum is far away and long ago, entirely useless from any practical point of view, but knowledge of a town from the practical viewpoint is a narrow knowledge. I liked museums.

The museum of Friedheim was a low brick building two blocks east of the church. There was no one in it but an elderly woman clerk. She told me to call her if I wanted anything and, after that, she left me alone. An admirable woman! I walked amid an incredible jungle of string instruments, some of them very odd in appearance to a man of this century. Friedheim had been making musical instruments since 1677, or so a placard stated; violins, violas, cellos, guitars, plus some strange affairs that I could not name. There was a second museum room devoted to shoes, boots, and sandals. Friedheim had been making foot coverings for a longer time than it had been making fiddles and, evidently, it had made some fairly fancy shoes in its day. In the third room, amid early lamps and lanterns, swords and pikes and uniforms, was the truly great exhibit.

They had the wagon in which corpses were hauled during the Black Death in 1632.

The wagon was crudely made with four solid wheels. It was designed to be pulled by a single animal and it had the shape of an open box. It might have held eight or ten bodies if they were piled high but six was the more likely limit. The surface of the wood was rough and there were spots where rot had attacked it but, once the decision was reached to preserve this wagon it was placed in the hands of men who knew and understood wood. It existed still and the generations of men who tended it were gone.

The museum was quiet, dimly lighted in this back room. I stood looking at the plague wagon and the Black Death became very real to me. I remembered accounts that I had read. The accounts were of England, of London mainly, but they could have been from anywhere on the continent where the millions had died. I could hear the creaking of wagon wheels and see the dimly lighted streets. Men had walked beside the plague wagons and their voices had echoed clamorously:

"Bring out your dead!"

The survivors, if there were survivors, had the choice of retaining the deadly, infectious corpses of their loved ones, already turning black, or of hauling them down to the street and a place in a heaped-up wagon.

It could not have been much different in this small town than in the big cities; fewer dead, perhaps, but high in proportion. They might, or might not, have found it necessary to sound their cry, "Bring out your dead!"

I shook my head and turned away. That ugly wagon

made it all quite real. I prided myself normally on a controlled detachment, a noninvolvement in the emotional affairs or experiences of others. I was not detached.

The clerk at the desk in the front room looked up inquiringly when I entered her domain. "I have been looking at the plague wagon," I said. "It carried the victims of the plague through the streets of this town. Could you tell me which streets it moved on and where it took the bodies?"

"I was not here." She shrugged slightly. "It moved on all the streets, that wagon. So I would think. It went down Gebetstrasse to the pits."

"Could I find where these pits were?"

"Yes. The pits are at the end of the street. Gebetstrasse goes eastward, past the church."

"Thank you."

It did not surprise me that everything in this town centered in the church, or began there, or ended there. It was inevitable. I walked up the slight hill from the museum and once more the church confronted me, a church like a great many others, with an onion-shaped steeple. I walked past it, heading eastward and found myself on Gebetstrasse. It was one of the streets that Judas had described as old, a quiet street of old-fashioned houses with projecting gables and occasional corner windows. In four blocks I put the houses behind me and there were two more blocks of cobbled streets with no structures of any kind. At the end of those two blocks there was a flat field without trees or shrubs or vegetation. This was the plague pit.

The bleakly flat space was sixty or seventy yards wide and thirty yards deep. The villagers had covered the area with gravel, probably within a short time after the plague had abated, and had kept that gravel renewed. I did not know how deep that covering went but it was unyielding beneath my feet and I had an eerie feeling as I walked it.

Long ago, centuries ago, men from this village had dug a trench here. They had not dug it, certainly, until the plague was sweeping through Friedheim. The need for it existed then. Many of the diggers probably died of the plague before it was over, and the men who drove the wagon, hauling the dead to this spot and rolling them out into the ditch.

Standing there, I could see it. They would pick up the dead at night. There would be torches, smoky torches, and quite possibly a fire burning beside the ditch, or in it. Those people of the seventeenth century believed that the Black Death avoided fire, that fire would keep it away if one used it properly. So there would be fire here to keep the plague in this bleak field with the people it had killed, to keep it from coming back into the village.

I could see it, see all of it.

There was a low ancient wall beyond the gravel, a wall that acted as a back boundary. The years and the weather had taken toll of the stone. There was the remnant of a statue in mid-wall and from the contour one could tell that this had been a pieta but no detail of the mother or of the dead son in her lap had survived.

I walked back on the parallel street to Gebetstrasse and found myself on a street of shoes; of shops with shoe-shaped signs and open fronts, cobblers laboring within the shops. It was a short street with an impressively long name, Flickschusterstrasse. There was a circle at the end of the street with a small fountain and a venerable bronze image of a saint, a thin, worried-looking saint with a beard as full as any of those in town. He had something in his left hand that looked like an awl. His right hand was raised in blessing. In the base below him there was an identifying line. Age had dulled it but it could still be read: SAINT KRISPIN.

It was an interesting name but I had never heard of him. I was walking away when I remembered the awl and the street of shoe shops. Of course. This was, undoubtedly, the patron saint of cobblers. The museum had told me of Friedheim's shoe-making past and the evidence was before me that the ancient craft still survived, even if overshadowed by stringed instruments.

There was a one-block street leading southward from the statue. I could not find the name of it but it was a very old street, cobbled. The houses were two-story, row-houses with no space dividing them. There were bronze devices above the doorways and in the separating space between windows, the heads of men, of lions, of gargoyles. At one time the heads had had meaning, of course, each a symbol of something, but it would be difficult to recapture the meaning now; probably impossible, as it was impossible to translate the messages scattered so profusely through old cathedrals. Fascinated, as I have always been, by heads of bronze, this was my street. I walked the length of it and back. It would be a street to sketch.

This was the old section of town, one of the oldest streets, dating to a time before the plague, before the Swedes, before the first Passion Play. Boniface Rohlmann, who had been thirteen years old when the Swedes came, and the plague, had known this street, had walked on it.

"They were not an outstanding family," Judas had said of the Rohlmanns. Quite possibly, then, they had lived on this street which was not outstanding either. One of them had been one of the great painters of his time, whether the family knew it or not, whether the world knew it or not. The world still did not know.

I walked the length of the street again. It was a quiet street. Nothing moved on it and I was not aware of any peering eyes from windows although the eyes were undoubtedly there. There was a house at the halfway point of the block with the head of a Jester above the door. It was a bronze that dated probably from a time when there were Jesters although Friedheim was an unlikely place in which to find one. The face under the peaked cap was that of a man with no illusions, a man with a smile as elusive as that of the Mona Lisa. His eyes were closed but his face, without the aid of eyes, was eloquent. A Jester, by tradition, was of admittedly low station but gifted with understanding of the limitations of those above him. This one was the symbol of his entire guild.

"Boniface Rohlmann lived here," I decided, "in this house. It would be perfect for him."

It was an arbitrary conclusion, of course, without the support of a single fact but it satisfied me. The boy who lived here had known the horror of the Black Death, the excitement and the terror of invading soldiers. The boy found, somewhere and somehow, the means to go away, to study painting, to produce at least one masterpiece and, unquestionably, other fine paintings which had mysteriously vanished. It was almost possible to imagine him walking behind me on the silent street and I had to restrain the impulse to look back.

The conviction grew on me that Neil Carlton had selected the least qualified man that he could find for this mission to a holy and industrious town. I lacked the solid, sober, steady temperament of a scientific investigator. I was unstable, a creature of fancies, a rider on vaporous clouds of imagination. *Sphere* would not employ me to empty wastebaskets.

Joan Terrill swept into the Bahnhof dining room when I was barely settled at my table. She was a girl who seemed, always, to move briskly and the touch of the open air was on her; fresh natural color in her cheeks, slight disorder in her hair. She was the soul and the spirit of improbability. No newspaper, or magazine, girl that I had ever known was even remotely like her.

"Mr. Donner, I must talk to you," she said. "May I sit at your table for a minute?"

The request was preposterous. Anyone else would have seated herself at the table. Her dark eyes were fixed on me and there was anxiety in them, a doubt perhaps that I would listen to her for a minute. She was a perfect antidote for that haunting plague pit. I wanted to listen to her.

"You are the answer to a prayer," I told her. "I have just come from the church where I said a novena, asking them to send me a pretty girl to share lunch with me."

"Them?" She was suddenly in command of herself again, scornful of me. "And a novena! A novena takes nine days or nine weeks. You never went near the church."

"How do you know?"

"I'm willing to bet."

"Fine." I handed her my menu. "You win the bet. You have just won a lunch with white wine."

The menu was a small card with a limited list of choices, as befitted the second hotel in a town like Friedheim. Joan Terrill accepted it automatically. She looked at it, obviously without seeing it.

"I am counting ten," she said. "As you could guess, I want something from you. I must be tactful and all that

but you are disconcerting. You put me at a terrible dis-
advantage. I nerved myself up to this. I was not seeking
an invitation to lunch."

"You weren't invited. You won the lunch. We will post-
pone your question until after the last of the wine. Then,
my answer will be 'Yes.' Simple? Relax."

"You don't know that your answer will be 'Yes'."

"I do. Certainly."

She shrugged slightly and in that moment she was, at
least a little, like a newspaper woman. "You asked for it,"
she said.

We studied our menus and we ordered our lunches.
Ordering was a serious business for her. She frowned over
it. I remembered her worrying about there being no driver
on the bus. Life, even in its trifling moments, would always
be real and earnest to her probably; a whole series of
tough, tall mountains to be climbed.

"I've been totaling up the things that I know about you,"
I said.

"You don't know anything about me."

"I know that you are a person who takes religion seriously, very seriously. You are, undoubtedly, a Roman
Catholic. Your name is Joan and you were unquestionably
named after Joan of Arc. You must be a good writer or
you would not be over here representing *Sphere*. You are
an attractive girl and you go around trying to mar the
effect. You are intolerant."

Her eyes were level to mine. She frowned slightly. "I
guess that I am expected to answer all of that."

"No. It isn't necessary."

"Then I will answer it for my own satisfaction. Not self-
defense, merely clarification."

"That is up to you."

"Right." She turned a wineglass in her hand, looking at it rather than at me. "I do take religion seriously because I believe in God. It is a link with Him. Other people in other religions have that link, maybe stronger links than I have. I don't know. I like the Catholic link. I am a believer."

She made a short slicing gesture with her right hand, cutting off that subject as finished. "I was named after Joan of Arc, as you suspected. My mother was devoted to her. She means something to me." Her eyes lifted to mine. "Something in your voice when you mentioned her expressed a degree of scorn, of denigration."

"I didn't know my voice was so revealing. I think that you overstate the case of how I feel."

"I am sensitive to voices."

"You must be. All right. Joan of Arc, to me, is a rather phony legend, built big by religious people and romantic people. I cannot feel her. I stood on the spot where they burned her to death in Rouen and I still could not feel her, nor any reality in her."

"I would like to visit Rouen. I know that I would feel her there." She shook her shoulders slightly. "Never mind. Next point. You are wrong. I am not a good writer. I am frightened to death by the writing side of this assignment. I am a research specialist and I am good at that."

There was a moment of silence while she twirled the wineglass again. I waited with easy patience. It was going to be interesting to see how she handled the next point.

"About my being attractive," she said slowly; "I won't be coy. I know that I am not hideous. I work on what I've got." Her eyes met mine again. "But I do not run around scattering bait for the males. Damned few of the males I've met are worth the bait. I keep my circles, male and female, small. As for being intolerant, I'll pass comment except to say that I consider toleration a patronizing thing. I have contempt for cheapness, irreverence, and vulgarity but I would not give that contempt the name of intolerance."

She surprised me with that outburst and the waitress bringing our lunch made a reply on my part unnecessary. The steward brought wine and then we were alone again.

"It's your turn," I said. "What do you know about me?"

She shook her head. "Nothing. I'm not permitting myself an opinion. I have a favor to ask."

"It has already been granted."

"I won't hold you to that. You may change your mind after you hear what I want."

"I won't."

We chatted across a table, saying nothing consequential. She had grown up in Cincinnati and I in St. Louis, people of the big rivers, both of us, if that meant anything. She laughed when I mentioned that and she had music in her laugh.

"I went to school in Cincinnati," she said, "and to college, to Mount St. Joseph-on-the-Ohio. We could look across into Kentucky from our campus. I was born, however, in Elkhart, Indiana. We had rivers there, too, and a big creek. Our town made musical instruments, all kinds. That's a link with Friedheim, isn't it?"

"A vague one."

"Not so vague." She dismissed the topic with a wave of her hand and leaned forward in her chair. "Now, about what I want. I'm losing my nerve."

"Don't! Let us have it."

"*Sphere* arranged for a photographer," she said, "a German from Munich. I have to use airmail and catch deadlines. I needed that photographer. I called him in Munich. He will not come until day after tomorrow. He says that *Sphere* does not pay enough, so he must be quick. He is probably right. *Sphere* would send a photographer from the United States with a big expense account or hire one over here and insist on a discount."

It was obvious now what she wanted but she had to lead up to it, slowly, hesitantly. She drew a deep breath. "I remembered that cow you sketched. I—well, would you do two sketches for me? For *Sphere,* that is. I'll make them pay you."

"Forget *Sphere*. I'll do them for you. When?"

"Right away. This afternoon. I have to mail them to-night."

"Of what?"

"Of Mr. Veit, the Apostle John, and one of the town, sort of a panorama or atmosphere picture."

Her inexperience was showing. She could not, of course, have the Jesus or the Mary for a picture until after the first performance; but she was making the John character too important by giving him a spot alone. He should have someone with him, perhaps Mary Magdalene or one of the bearded apostles. John was the only beardless one of the Jesus followers. Beards were typical of the town and the play and she was not providing one. She was enamored and she could not see that.

She would do better, too, with a picture of the rural theater, awkwardly big in relation to the town, rather than the town itself. It would be presumptuous for me to tell her such things. I was on a lower rung of the journalistic ladder, looking up at her.

"It will be a busy afternoon," I said. "Let us get started."

CHAPTER SIX

John was waiting for us at Joan Terrill's hotel. He was living testimony to the fact that she had never doubted her own powers. She had told him to be there and she knew that I would be there. All of which is an essay on women. I did not doubt at all that her nervousness and surface uncertainty had been genuine. A woman could *know* and still doubt, have faith in her own powers and still be aware of her limitations, see what she wanted as a reality yet worry over a possibility of failure in which she did not really believe. I had seen all of that many times. I had been married to a woman who was feminine if she was nothing else, a woman who could play the whole book without ever bothering to read the music.

John was a fairhaired youth with long curly hair. He was wearing a green robe and a pink mantle. He wore sandals with crisscrossed leather straps running up his calf, and he was built like an athlete, his skin smooth and deeply sun-bronzed. His eyes were pale blue and there was something in them that I did not like. As a matter of fact, there was little in the whole man that I liked. Despite his obvious physical fitness, he looked soft. I thought again, looking at him, that he needed someone in the scene with him, that he was nothing alone.

"How shall I pose him?" I asked Joan Terrill. "What is he doing? Where are we in the Passion Play?"

"He is writing," she said. "He was a writer. He should be sitting on that low fence, writing in a pad."

"They didn't have pens in those days. Writing with what?"

"A quill," she said calmly. "I brought one. Also a book. It is old and you can make it look older, I am certain."

It should, I was certain, be a scroll and not a book but I did not raise the point. We gave the Apostle John his tools and he seemed more interested in mine. It was difficult to get him away from the easel and the board and the pencils. I finally got him seated on the stone fence and I went to work.

John, once away from the easel, was an actor, born with the mystic something that places a man squarely in the middle of his make-believe world. I have lived through a period when I knew many actors, and actresses, and there was no longer any astonishment left in me where they were concerned. It did not surprise me in the least when John posed with the best side of his face in profile to me, his chin lifted, his hand with the quill poised gently above the book. He paid no attention to me. He was interested only in himself; which was, of course, the perfect formula for what we had to do.

A couple of lines from Elizabeth Barrett Browning ran through my head when I looked at John and blocked him out on the pad. They were two wonderfully rhythmic lines

which, somehow, had meaning at the moment and I could
not recall any lines beyond the two:

> What is he doing, the great god Pan,
> Down in the reeds by the river?

The great god Pan was posing, and posing beautifully.
His was a simple portrait to do and I had a difficult job
ahead of me, so I worked fast. In one pause I looked at
the girl. She was leaning forward, completely enthralled
with the physical beauty before her; not guarding herself
at all, fascinated by him. It was disturbing to see the rapt
look in her face. She was not aware of anybody or anything
except this character who played John.

"How can she be so involved?" I thought. "It is impossible in more ways than one."

That was not my concern nor my responsibility. Because
I did not want to fail such obvious happiness, I gave John
a full order of glamour, all of the charm of line and
feature, suppressing my impulse to sketch in some of the
inanity that I felt in him. When I finished I handed the
sketch to the girl. It was the kind of thing that the magazine could reproduce as easily as a photograph. Joan Terrill's eyes widened when she saw it.

"It is wonderful," she said. "Far, far better than I had
dared to hope."

Apostle John came over fast, looking down on the portrait past the girl's shoulder. "It is, isn't it?" he said. "Superb."

"So now I'll go up on the hill and get the town," I
said. "I'll be back in time for you."

She planned, I knew, to send the sketches, wrapped for
airmailing, to Munich on the last bus. She did not seem to

hear me. She and John were still admiring John's picture. I strode away from them and I did not look back.

The afternoon was warm and it was a hot uphill trip to my spot on the hillside from which I had studied the town on my first day. I set up my portable easel and my devoted cow strolled slowly over, her bell sounding. It was a welcome of sorts. None of the other cows paid any attention to me.

"I have no time for you today, Milky," I said. "I'm sorry about that, but you have had your portrait painted."

The animal stood and watched me, not chewing cud, not doing a thing, merely standing in one spot, holding an unblinking stare. Oddly, I liked having her there. She was company. It would be easy to believe that she liked me.

The town of Friedheim was spread out below me, with the sun strong on the red roofs, the shadow deep in the streets. This was the Middle Ages. I could paint the town as I saw it now and it would serve to illustrate any medieval tale. I would, of course, have to touch it up here and there and eliminate one anachronism. There were television aerials discreetly dispersed among the roofs, not so many as in an American town of this size but enough to command notice.

I sketched the shape of the town and I placed the church in its point of command and I worked in the other major spots, establishing their relationship to the church, a very real relationship of location and balance.

Here was the town of Friedheim. The people who came to see the Passion Play would walk in awe through the medieval streets, sit for hours under the tragic spell of the play, feel the holy atmosphere, watch the sacred drama and carry a picture away with them that was, perhaps, illusion more than truth. They would not be aware of the people in the houses, under the television aerials or those under the roofs that were without aerials. No matter how Friedheim looked in the streets, or from a high spot in the hills, the people who lived in the medieval houses were people who lusted and hated and coveted, people who engaged in malicious gossip, people greedy for money or for power, for a little money, perhaps, and a little power. There would be jealousies down there under the roofs and angers and perverted cravings; all the faults and weaknesses and human failings that one would find in any town, in whatever country one might search.

I, sitting on the hillside, was contributing to the perpetuation of legend. Holy, holy Friedheim! Well, why not? I could give them John, the Beloved Apostle, and a star-shaped town huddled around its church and give it to them honestly. Never mind what I believed or did not believe. I had no desire to look behind the discreetly drawn curtains of houses or the drawn curtains of lives.

The hours raced. I would have allowed three days, at least, for the sketching of the town. The galloping hours were all that I had. I needed to show the light which flamed across Friedheim and I was not working in oils. I obtained my light through its opposite, dealing carefully with the shadows. The low hills were awesome shapes on three sides of the star, sinking into obscurity at town level, climbing into light on the crests. The river flowed around a third of the town and there were two bridges.

I caught it all and it was a good piece of work, not remarkable but good. I was pleased with it when I signed off and packed to go down the hill. The cow had moved a few feet closer to me, still regarding me steadily, unblinkingly, not a creature given to speech or sound.

"You are a faithful mascot, Milky," I said, "and I appreciate it."

Joan Terrill was waiting at her hotel. She had her dispatches written and her package ready for the sketch. She looked at Friedheim as I had seen it and she seemed impressed as she had been impressed with John.

"It is marvelous," she said. "I had no idea that you were so good. I am embarrassed. I had no right to ask you. I have told *Sphere* that they must send you a check. I hope they send you enough." She made a helpless, feminine, two-handed gesture. "You have no idea how grateful I am."

"The fun was all mine," I said. "Now get those things on the bus."

She had had more appeal, even if only a trifle more, when she was crisp, detached, above and beyond the use of superlatives. John had been responsible for the melting and it was not becoming to her. I went down to the Eisenhut to meet Judas Iscariot. He was waiting for me but he already had his beer, a half-filled stein on the small table before him.

"I hope that you have not paid for that," I said.

He shook his head. "It would have been a folly if you were to come. You would be offended."

"I certainly would."

"*Ja.*"

There was a gleam of humor in his eye. I remembered his wife saying: "My husband, Josef, is a very fine actor." and, "God has given him a great gift, perhaps, because he has need of it." This man who played Judas had little money, probably, and earned little. It could, conceivably, mean something to him if someone bought his beer. The boy brought my stein and I lifted it in salute to the man across the table.

"I have seen most of your town and I like it."

"What, in the town, did you like?"

"The fact that it is shaped like a star."

"You discovered that, did you? Few tourists do."

"I am not a tourist. The tourists would discover it if the town mentioned the fact in its literature."

Judas shook his head. "It is always better for people to discover facts for themselves. Always better. The facts mean more. That star is a strange thing. The town was not always shaped like that. No one could have planned it. None of us can remember who first discovered it, or when."

"There are a lot of strange things about your town. I visited the plague pit."

"That is not strange. It was a necessity. It is there."

"I walked over it. It did something to me emotionally. Why? Millions of people have died all over the world since 1632. Why should those strangers in the ground mean anything to me? Anything at all?"

Judas took out his pipe and was leisurely in the filling of it. "It is not the dying of strangers that affects us," he said. "It is being close to their deaths."

"What is that? Say that again."

He shook his head. "It is not necessary. You will remember. Did you visit the old streets?"

"Yes. The violin section and the shoe section."

"Busy streets. Good craftsmen. Our business in Friedheim is small but our people make things well."

"I am certain that they do. I found a small street without a name. There is a house with a Jester's head above the door, an excellently done head. The idea came to me that Boniface Rohlmann might have been born there, that he lived there."

"It is possible. The house is very old. Hans Aschenbrenner lives there now. He is a Roman soldier in the play. As I told you, Rohlmanns did live in Friedheim once. There have been wars, invasions, two bad fires. The ancient records in my office are fragments, mostly supplied by the old families who kept their own records."

"If I talked to some of them, the old families, might they have some record of the Rohlmanns?"

"No. I have all that they have. The town made a great effort." Judas puffed thoughtfully on his pipe. "There is a source. It would do you little good. You are not a Catholic?"

"No."

"You would have to be a Catholic. The pastor of this parish church, Father Albrecht Schecker, has many records. No one knows how many. Churches learn to protect things, you understand. There are vaults, crypts, secret places. The town does not have secrets from the church and on secrets the church is discreet."

"There is no need for discretion, certainly, in the life of a painter who has been dead for centuries."

"There might be. At any rate, the priest would tell you nothing."

"You are a good Catholic. You ask him."

Judas laughed into his empty stein and I ordered him another beer. "Between the good father and me there is friendship. There is also relationship, a communicant and his pastor. In the field of information about Friedheim, there is perhaps competition. He feels that history reposes with him. He would give me none of it."

This was a situation which I could not have imagined;

yet, confronted with it, I could see clearly how it would be. Knowing that data had been preserved in a place just beyond my reach was maddening; a condition more infuriating than the blank of no data.

"He may have little that you would want. He may have nothing at all," Judas said. "His church had a fire, too, and it knew the wars."

"He would not talk to me? You are certain of that?"

"He would talk to you. He is a gentleman, the priest, a pleasant man; but he would tell you nothing."

"I will have to find a way past that."

Judas laughed again. "The street of the house with the Jester is Kirschbaumstrasse. The number is 18. The house is three hundred years old at least, perhaps fifty years more. That little street was there when the Swedes came. That is three hundred and fifty years."

Judas was speaking with greater deliberation now and I realized that my own faculties had slowed. We had had three beers and those big steins were deep.

"You were thinking about the plague pit," he said slowly. "In the history of Friedheim only one witch was burned to death. That is where they burned her. Her name was Frieda Neuhardt. It was in 1661."

I did some startled mental arithmetic. "They performed the Passion Play here in 1662," I said.

"Yes."

"How could pious people, dedicated people, people carrying out a vow, burn a woman to death? A neighbor probably."

Judas drew hard on his pipe. He was a broad, blocky man and his features within the framework of the black beard were strong features.

"There is Evil," he said simply.

He made the flat statement and let it lie without elaboration. One could reason if one would that he was recognizing the evil in human beings who would burn a woman to death, but I did not interpret him in that sense. Evil to him was a four-letter word and the "E" was a capital letter. (In German, too, evil is a four-letter word—*übel*—and his intonation capitalized the "u.")

I thought about Judas as I walked with a slight unsteadiness to my hotel. There was a fine misty rain falling and I had a fine mist in my brain so my thoughts did not track clearly.

It was natural perhaps for a man who believed in an ultimate "Good," a creator, a saviour, a promise of eternal life, to believe also in the opposite; in ultimate Evil, a destroyer, a betrayer, a threat of annihilation. Good, with all of its churches and its prophets and its priests, was a dealer often in shoddy charity, in smug hypocrisy, in flexible codes of morality, in cruelty, in falsehood, in smug self-indulgences. Evil, without aspirations, without an exalted concept to serve, offering no check on man's animal nature and no reward for his spirit was a monstrous thing to contemplate.

I did not believe in either good or evil, with small letters or with capitals.

It was interesting that I now had a lead to Boniface Rohlmann, a direction in which to move from a position which had seemed dead center. The priest of Friedheim had records to which the town had access only at his discretion; the early history of families, perhaps, the births and the marriages and the deaths. There would be scandals, no doubt, and outrageous things but they were things of the long ago involving people dead and forgotten, people unknown to the reader of records. One would say that all of this was history and belonged in the open, but a small-town priest in Germany occupied a place of power. One did not ride over him or around him.

All of this mental circumlocution reached ultimately the point that I did not want to reach. There was a girl who was a devout Roman Catholic. She was also a trained researcher. She was a girl for whom I had just done a favor and from whom I did not want to ask any favors in return. I could walk a road of irony to some knowledge of Boniface Rohlmann or I could fold up and go home.

There was a letter waiting for me at the hotel. It was from Neil Carlton. He had written it obviously before he received my letter and, in typical Carlton fashion, he discussed all of the people and affairs which did not matter before he reached the two points of significance, the least of those, of course, came first.

Father Graney has never got over that night of the painting (he wrote). He has taken an unreasonable dislike to Ludwig and he dismisses the very real mystery of that night as a lot of "Hocus Pocus," of what he calls "Lorenson Claptrap." He closes his eyes to all the reality of that soul-shaking experience and when I attempted to discuss his contentions reasonably, he blew up and told me that he expected better of me, that I was allowing myself to be taken in by a lot of gypsy fakery, that I had left my mind and my God-given reason in the, and I quote, "Lorenson Seance Room." I fear, Kirk, that I have lost a friend and I know that Ludwig has lost one. It distresses me greatly.

Of more saddening impact is the news that I have saved for last. And of plain cowardice, I have shrunk from the reporting. Robert Maxwell died last night. For a great many years he was merely "Robert" to me and that sufficed; a man of humor and trust and a great dignity. I was sincerely fond of him and I respected him. I owe to you my first knowledge that his name was Maxwell. As Robert, or as Robert Maxwell, he was someone in my life whom I always enjoyed seeing. I do not say that of too many people. He died quietly in his sleep last night and Ludwig is upset beyond all reason. He says that I killed him, that Robert would still be healthy, happy and alive if I had not shown him that painting.

I do not know if you will ever discover anything about the painting or the man who painted it. It doesn't matter, Kirk. It doesn't matter. I wish that none of us had ever seen it.

Devotedly

Neil.

I sat for a long while in the dark with that letter. The rain was pattering against the window panes and, far away, thunder was rolling through the hills. I had lost a friend. I remembered little jokes in an elevator, laughter and warmth and genuine liking, the rich joy of that Christmas when I brought Robert the portrait I had painted: Robert at the wheel of an old Maxwell.

Robert was dead. Sitting in my room, with the thunder and the rain as background, I heard his voice again, a shocked voice protesting what, to him, had been betrayal:

"Mr. Donner, it isn't right to do this to me. I wouldn't shake my fist at my Lord and my God."

I did not know if Robert had ever lost that initial belief of his, the belief that I had painted him into that canvas of Boniface Rohlmann's. I hated the thought that he had died believing that.

I hated the idea, too, of Ludwig believing that Neil Carlton was responsible for Robert's death. Neil's motivation in bringing Robert to see the painting had been complicated but I understood it if Ludwig did not. To believe that

that painting had caused Robert's death was equivalent,
perhaps, to attributing evil to the painting itself. That could
be true only if one believed death to be an evil. Robert was
a man who lived in pain and with illness. Death, perhaps,
had been kind. How was one to know?

Moving in such murky corridors of speculation as this
was unpleasant to me, foreign to my habit. I gestured
violently with my right hand, brushing all intangibles away.
Robert was dead. That was the simple fact; final, complete,
beyond any need of explanation or of blame.

In the end I wrote a letter, a long letter, not to Neil
Carlton who had provided a measure of healing to his own
pain when he wrote to me, but to Ludwig Lorenson who
had denied himself sympathy by alienating the people who
offered it to him.

I walked to the post office in the rain and I became
thoroughly wet in the walking. In that there was an in-
definable spiritual peace. I, who scoffed at all clumsy, ar-
tificial man-made attempts to invoke the spiritual, wel-
comed the peace that came to me.

BOOK TWO
The Play

CHAPTER ONE

Saturday was the day of the play, the first performance. It was a morning of pale sunlight after a day and a night of rain. There were two Masses at 6 A.M., one in the church and one in the auditorium. Practically every human being in Friedheim was at one Mass or the other. I ate my breakfast at the hotel. A few of the correspondents who came down on Friday were having breakfast, too. They were strangers and I was not interested in them. At that hour of the morning I was not even interested in myself.

It had been a brutally wet day on Friday; a whistling wind and continuous rain. Correspondents from all over Germany, from France, Belgium, the Netherlands, and Italy came damply, grumpily into town. The Saturday showing of the play was primarily for them; it would not open for the general public until Monday when, if it was lucky, it would arrive in sunshine. There was a tense atmosphere in the town Saturday morning, an electric something which even a resister such as I could feel. The church bells rang at six to announce that the Mass was about to begin and, to my surprise, they rang happily. I had expected solemn, if not doleful music and not the cheery note.

They rang again at seven, still brightly resonant. I did not want to watch the Mass crowd eating breakfast, so I got out early. I walked to the plague pit for no particular reason, and dropped a thought in it for the woman who had died there as a witch. I was early at the theater, glad of the chance to appreciate its awesome emptiness.

"If you were not of the press," a solemn functionary said, "you would not be admitted to the theater until a half hour before the performance."

"A free press is the joy and the glory of any country," I said, with equal solemnity.

The man blinked at me and I hoped that he would spend the morning digesting my remark. It was a huge theater, mostly of wood construction with its suggestion of fire hazard. My guidebook said that it would hold three thousand people, about half the size of the one at Oberammergau and probably optimistic in being so large.

Joan Terrill joined me while the hall was still sparsely populated. She was excited, not at all surprised to find herself seated beside me. The joker at the press relations desk had obviously told her how smart he was, discovering that there were two Americans and deciding that they should sit together.

"You weren't at the Mass," she said.

"No. Did you believe that I would be?"

"It was, I thought, possible. You missed something. It was the perfect preparation for the play."

"I'm prepared."

She looked away from me, looking down at the slowly filling seats below us. We sat high and center. There was a succession of seating areas, rising gradually. The second area in which we were sitting was unquestionably the best.

Something about this girl, even when she was being

pleasant, triggered me into the boorish and the crude. There was no point to that.

"I am glad that I have this seat and that you have the one beside me," I said.

The girl flashed one look in my direction, then away. "Are you?"

"Yes."

"That makes everything easier. I was pleased when I learned about the seating. I hate to watch anything alone and I am not good with strangers." She made an odd gesture with her right hand. "Of course you are a stranger actually but you were so nice about doing those sketches for me. You do not seem like a stranger."

I shrugged. "There are more people here than I expected. They are going to fill the place."

She laughed softly. "You do not like thanks, do you? Or praise? That is interesting. Neither do I. There are a lot of people here because the families of people in the cast, and of everyone connected with the play, have invitations to the press preview. This performance belongs to the town really; more so than to the press."

"I did not know that."

Again, the girl had done her homework better than had I. She was not, of course, haunted by the ghost of Boniface Rohlmann as I was; still, I should have done better.

The thought of Rohlmann intruded on this day. I had to use this girl to reach even a glimmer of information about the man and I did not want to do it. I could not ask certainly on the day of the all-important play.

The director of the orchestra came in quietly without taking a bow and there was a sudden hush before music answered his baton. It was soft music, as cheerful as the church bells had been but laced with a hint of foreboding.

Angels moved swiftly, glidingly, onto the stage, singing, and all of this was prelude. The curtain rose slowly.

We, in the audience, had a roof over our heads; the stage and the performers had none. It was a large stage with its own sets and effects but behind it were the Friedheim hills. The out-of-doors flowed onto the stage and the audience, facing south, did not have to contend with intense light.

People, the people of a village, young and old, moved on the stage, people with colorful mantles and robes. They were in the streets of a town and there was an arched town gate of simulated stone. Another group of people flowed through that gate and the central figure was riding a small donkey. The crowd hailed him joyously and he raised his hand in a greeting or a blessing.

This was the Christ and I was startled at how faithfully he fulfilled the traditional portraits. This was a living man, not a concept. He smiled, spoke to individuals, patted the heads of children, happy to be among people who liked him.

The scene changed swiftly when he reached the temple. The money changers were busy there and he ordered them out, overturning tables and counters when they defied him. A lot of temple people, including some whom I took to be rabbis, came to the defense of the money changers and the people came behind Christ, calling out: "Hosanna to the Son of David!"

It was a bit melodramatic but the girl beside me was tensely involved in it. I saw her boy, John, in the group around Jesus. Judas was there, too: mob-members, both of them, with nothing much to do.

I liked the scene where the temple people and the traders met in a stormy session. They were plainly outspoken.

They did not believe that Christ had the right or the authority to interfere with people or procedures in the temple and, on the evidence, it seemed to me they had a point. They decided that Christ was a menace to all of them, a prophet out of the North who was dangerous because he had the people with him.

"He must be stopped now," one of them said. "There are people coming into the town who have not heard him. They are not his followers. He must be arrested and tried for many crimes: heresy, blasphemy, transgressions which those people do not love."

"How arrested?" someone said.

"At night. Someone must point him out to the temple guards. Not one of us!"

"I know the very man," a character named Dathan said, "one of his followers! The fellow needs money. His name is Judas."

"A modern playwright could not do anything better than that," I said. "That scene sets up everything. Those plotters sound like people of our own time."

Joan Terrill was sitting with her clenched fists in her lap. She did not answer me. On the stage the plotters were gone and Christ was visiting with his followers, planning to go to Bethany for the Passover. He was a Christ that I did not expect, one that none of the great painters caught, one not described in the Gospels. He was the companion, talking with close friends, planning a trip. There was no spoken dialogue after the first few exchanges, the men laughing and talking in pantomime. They were like men anywhere, enjoying the day and the company of one another.

"A laughing Christ!" I said. "It never occurred to me. That is what religion has always needed."

Joan Terrill ignored that comment as she had ignored the others. Nothing existed for her except what was happening on the stage. I, too, felt the strange reality of the performance but I lived simultaneously in two worlds.

The scenes flowed swiftly. Some of them were awkward scenes and some of the dialogue was painfully clumsy; but one could feel the tightening tension of the audience as the drama built. The character of Judas was growing, gaining strength, and the man was a superb actor. It was not believable that I had ever loafed at a table, drinking beer with him.

Judas wore a yellow robe and a dull orange mantle, a villainous costume that was as obvious as a black hat in a cowboy drama. He was the villain but he played the full range, not content to be melodramatically villainous. He had a soliloquy comparable to Hamlet's when he was first disturbed that Christ had, seemingly, no intention of re-establishing a new, prosperous, powerful Kingdom of Israel, that Christ spoke instead of parting and of death.

"I have had enough of hoping and of waiting," the restless Judas said. "There is nothing ahead of me but continual poverty and misery. I have known that all of my life. Perhaps it would be good to leave him while there is still time. His Kingdom of Glory I wished to share with him—but it comes not—and what comes? Misery and poverty. Who desires to share that with him? Not I. Not I."

There was raw power in Judas in that scene and in the one where Dathan cautiously explores his willingness to identify Christ for the soldiers.

The curtain dropped and when it rose again, Christ and his apostles were seated at a long table. It was Leonardo da Vinci's *The Last Supper* in every detail. Christ had blessed the bread and the wine, proclaimed it his body and blood and announced that one of those at the table would betray him. The apostles were shocked and horrified, calling out to him.

That scene held motionless on the stage for a full two minutes, a pale light playing over it.

The actors moved and spoke again. They were proclaiming it impossible that one of his friends would betray him.

"Name him! Name the man, Master!"

"Is it I, Master?" Judas said.

Another voice cut across his. "Who is it, Lord?" Christ dipped bread in wine.

"He to whom I give this sop."

Judas, at that moment, rose and left the table, left it rather magnificently, making no particular point of the leaving. The other apostles, calling out their queries and protests to Christ, seemed to draw no significance from the leaving.

The curtain came down.

When the curtain rose again, Judas and Dathan were before Caiphas. It was the scene in which Judas accepted the thirty pieces of silver and he appeared detestable in it, an avaricious man forgetful of friendship.

"Let your men come to the garden where he prays," Judas said. "They must have torches and lanterns. I will give them a sign."

The garden was another painting.

Christ in the garden. Jesus Christ knelt, his hands against a rock, his head back and his eyes lifted to the sky above him. Around him on the ground his disciples slept. For a minute the painting held, then Christ moved and we were back in the play.

"Father," he prayed, "if thou wilt, remove this chalice from me; but yet not my will but Thine be done."

It was the rather desperate prayer of a lonely man who was facing torture and death. Other voices sounded in the distance and then the temple guards came into the garden, following Judas. Christ came slowly to his feet. Judas walked up to him and kissed him.

"Friend, wherefore art thou come?" Christ said. "Betrayest thou the Son of Man with a kiss? Whom seek ye?"

"Jesus of Nazareth," a guard said.

"I am he."

The scene exploded into violence as the guards laid their hands on Jesus and the Apostles awakened. Peter drew his sword and cut the ear of someone named Malchus. The famous line of Christ was beautifully timed.

"Peter, put thy sword into the sheath. They that take the sword shall perish by the sword."

It was the end of an act, the end of the first half of the play. The curtain came down, and the church bells in the town tolled solemnly. Joan Terrill shook her head.

"It is wonderful," she said, "just wonderful."

"It pretty nearly is," I agreed.

The correspondents were moving into the aisles. There was no levity in them. Their faces were interesting, but I was more interested in the faces of the villagers. Faces are my first interest as an artist and these were great faces. The villagers of Friedheim had grown up with this drama. They had lived with the play, had known it through all of their lives as a legend of their town; but the play was not a commonplace to them. They had been stirred emotionally and the stirring showed in their faces.

"I ordered lunch and a table for two at my hotel," Joan Terrill said. "I hope that you will join me."

Her voice was not quite steady and there was a huskiness in it. I could understand that.

"Thank you," I said. "It is a pleasant thought."

I walked with her to the hotel and we had a table for two against the wall. She was a pretty girl; brown eyes of a strange intensity, a straight nose that was a trifle short, a mouth that seemed, in this relaxed moment, vulnerable.

"Are you really an unbeliever," she asked, "or is that a pose?"

"I try not to pose. The question is difficult to answer. Unbeliever in what?"

"In religion. In faith. In all that we were watching today."

She was so solemn that I was tempted to be facetious.

I brushed the temptation aside. "Let us drop that ugly word, 'unbeliever'! I have no religious belief. I could never accept what was told to me in the name of religion. The obvious myths always became mixed up with the admirable moral principles. Faith? That is another matter. I have had faith in many things. Today? The play far exceeded anything that I anticipated."

My voice seemed to run on and on. I never would have planned so long a speech. The girl listened. I could not read her eyes.

"These are real people, human beings," she said. "Some of them are cobblers, some cut leather, some carve wood and some make violins. They are not actors. Today they have made real to me a story that I have believed in all of my life, more real than it has ever been—and it has always been very real."

"You are fortunate, fortunate in having stories in which you can believe."

She shook her shoulders, a gesture too abrupt to be described as a shrug. "I did not mean to be so humorless.

Forgive me. We should talk of other things during this time away from the play. What shall we talk about?"

"You."

She laughed. She had a pleasant laugh. "There isn't much. You know most of it. I am on my first big assignment and afraid that I am not up to it. If I seemed odd that first day on the bus, that's the why of it. I was trying to be important and not certain that I was."

"You were all right. You worried about too many things. What would you do if you had free choice, could do anything you choose?"

Her forehead creased slightly then smoothed. "Just what I'm doing. I love research and on *Sphere* the rummaging for facts is never dull. I have never done anything that I have enjoyed as much as this assignment. I hope that I qualify for another."

"Again you are fortunate," I said.

"Yes. Very. Aren't you?"

"In many ways, yes."

"And in many ways, no, obviously. I'd like to hear either side of the coin; the fortunate or the unfortunate."

"You'd be bored."

"No. You forget that I love research."

Suddenly, for no sane reason, I wanted to do that most absurd of things, talk to a girl about me.

"I'll wrap the two sides of the coin together in a thin narrative," I said. "I am an artist. That is fortunate. I have never seriously wanted to be anything else. I have a yen to do portraits, to do them my way. Nobody wants what I like best to do. That is unfortunate."

"What kind of portraits do you want to do?"

"I want to do heads. I would do them on canvas but they would look like ancient bronze. I would do you, for instance, as you would have been done in the Middle Ages. You could see how you would look in bronze or stone on a cathedral portal."

"Heavens!" Her eyes widened. "I can see why people would not want that."

"You really can't. You would be beautiful, as you are. The faces on choir stalls, in all of the odd corners of old cathedrals, are marvelous faces, far better done on an average than the pretentious portraits in oil which are so widely acclaimed."

She laughed again. "I do not believe that you are unfortunate at all. You know what you want to do. But bronze faces! How did you ever decide on such a specialty?"

"One doesn't decide. An interest develops. It grows. One becomes committed to it. I know a painter, a very fine painter, who paints merry-go-round horses. He does them magnificently. He draws meaning, sometimes strange meaning, from them."

"I don't know whether to believe you," she said. "Merry-go-round horses!"

"You have never looked at one, really looked at it. A good one. The finest carrousel horses in the world are German but they are vanishing. My friend travels all over Germany seeking them—and he is an Englishman who hates Germans."

It was a strange topic to be discussing with a girl and I could tell from her puzzled expression that she was not following me on that tangent. She looked across the dining room and then her eyes came back to me.

"Are you married?" she said.

"I was."

"Was?"

"Yes. She divorced me."

"Oh!"

Her "oh" was a falling note. She was a Roman and divorce was one of the dirty words. I had put the fact as it was and the fact that Alicia had divorced me was a damning thing to the girl across the table, the fixing of a nameless guilt. It would take a rather long explanation to set the impression straight and there was no room in my slender relationship with this girl for long explanations. As if to emphasize that point, the church bell rang. It was time to start back to the play.

"I enjoyed the lunch," I said, "and the company. Will you have dinner with me tonight?"

She hesitated. "May I have a raincheck? Another time?"

"Certainly."

There was a shadow between us as we walked the narrow, winding streets to the auditorium. The hills were only dimly defined, the sky overcast. We found our seats and settled in. The tense expectancy of the crowd was contagious. I was feeling it in my nerves.

The play opened with a scene involving Annas, Esdras, and some of the other enemies of the Christ. These were men who obviously considered him a false prophet and an impostor. He was a menace to their own positions and their comfort but that was not their sole reason for disliking him.

Judas came in, wrapped in praise for doing well what he had been paid to do. Christ had been arrested and Annas said now of the arrest: "Even before the Feast, the Galilean shall die!"

Judas recoiled. It was the first time that he had heard of a death threat to Jesus Christ. He had acted in the belief that the arrest was planned to prevent Christ from stirring up the people during the High Holidays. He blinked now and shook his head.

"Die? Die?" he said. "No! I did not wish that. I do not. I did not deliver him up to you for that."

The men in the room looked at him with silent contempt. He cringed as his eyes swept the group. Annas dismissed him with a lordly gesture.

"Thou didst deliver him to us. What follows is our affair."

Once more, Judas was magnificent. He was ringed by hostile men who had no respect for him, an insignificant human tool who was no longer important to the people who had used him. He voiced his protest and it fell emptily. He could not erase what he had done nor change the direction of events that were in motion, but in his helplessness he was moving.

There were court scenes and tedious detail as Christ, playing the most dramatic of all roles, a man walking under a certain doom, faced his accusers; then Judas came back for one scene, flinging the thirty pieces of silver at the men who had bribed him and stalking out. His last soliloquy as he prepared to kill himself was the longest speech in the play. He paced the stage with it and his voice had thunder in it.

"I am proud that I knew him," I said to Joan Terrill. She looked at me startled. She was in the play, living the play, back two thousand years in time. I could not possibly know Judas and nobody could be proud of him. I conceded the point with a vague gesture. She was too far away from me for speech.

The movement of the play from Caiphas to Herod to Pilate, forward and back was tensely knit drama but I was only mildly interested. Joan Terrill was leaning forward, toward the stage, seeing nothing beyond it or apart from it. When Christ was flogged and exhibited on Pilate's balcony with the blood on his hands and his face, she was actually weeping. The crowd cried out: "His blood be upon us and upon our children," and I thought of Ludwig Lorenson. He had been correct. The cry meant, "All of us and the children of all of us."

There was a brief pause, a lowered curtain and then the curtain lifted again. I stiffened in my seat. It was another picture, the actors motionless for the minute in their roles.

The Roman soldiers, on an arc, were trying to push the crowd back and the crowd was resisting them. Christ was standing in the middle of the courtyard, blood on his mantle, blood in his hair. His legs were braced, slightly apart. The stage was open under the sky and there was a low hill, Pilate's balcony on the right, the crowd on the lower left. Christ was standing in the middle of the diagonal, in the natural painter-placing of the central figure. Men, women, and children menaced him, shaking fists, bending for stones to throw.

It was the painting of Boniface Rohlmann, exact in its every detail.

The painting flowed into the play and the characters were in motion, their voices raised in abuse. Instinctively I sought myself in the third row, knowing how absurd that was. There were people there but they were mere units in a mob, a mob that the Roman soldiers pushed out of the way. They took Christ off stage and the painting was gone.

"How could it be?" I thought. "How could it possibly be?"

Christ carried his cross and was, seemingly, nailed to

it in a graphic scene. He hung on that cross for twenty minutes. Ultimately, out of all of it, he rose from the dead and the angel voices of the choir sang in exultation. I followed it with only part of my mind. When I rose to leave the theater I was as dazed, as emotionally numb, as the people who moved down the aisle with me. Joan Terrill looked up into my face.

"It meant something to you after all, didn't it?" she said.

I drew a deep breath. "Yes," I said. "It certainly did."

We were two people speaking in different languages, not communicating at all, but that made no difference, no difference whatever.

CHAPTER TWO

Mardi Gras moved into Friedheim on Saturday night. The day had been long, a day of intense emotion, of sorrow, of joyous triumph. The Saviour had been arrested, tried, tortured, killed. He had risen from the dead. The people of the town were of peasant stock, simple people, supplying instinctively their own correctives to emotional situations. The morrow would be Sunday and tourists would be pouring in. The official opening of the Passion Play would be on Monday and the play would run through the summer. There would be no public exhibitions, dances, "pagan frivolity" during the time when strangers were in Friedheim to witness the Passion of the Lord. Saturday night was the night to vent one's feelings.

Dinner would be late and haphazard, for most people. There were men and women at tables in my hotel drinking beer. Voices were raised and there was much laughter. There were three fiddlers in the dining room who played lively music to which young people, and old, danced in any available space. I saw people whom I recognized. Pontius Pilate was there, talking to two women, a tall, handsome man, one of the few unbearded ones. In private

life Pontius Pilate was a chemist, proprietor of the drug-
store. Caiphas was sitting at a table with three other people.
He was laughing, a much more attractive man than he
seemed in the play.

Outside the hotel there was a single violinist standing
beside the fountain of the three children. A dozen or so
young people danced around him. In the cleared place
before Die Geiger a larger group danced. The old man
holding a violin looked down on them from the 1667
bronze. There were three instruments playing. I entered
the hotel and it was livelier there than at Bahnhof. The
only character I recognized was Nicodemus.

Joan Terrill was seated in one of the booths against
the wall, the same booth she had occupied the last time
I saw her in this room. She was sharing a table with the
same companion, the Beloved Apostle. They were not
noticing anyone else.

Outside there were people in all of the streets, some of
them in colorful costumes. Another group danced to the
music of a string quartet at the Town Hall fountain.

It was colorful and interesting to a point but I was an
actor without a role. There was no one with whom I
could share any of this Mardi Gras activity, no nonsense
in which I could participate without feeling ridiculous.

Inevitably I went to the Eisenhut. The long dimly lighted
room was misty with tobacco smoke, heavy with the odor
of tobacco and beer. Men and women sat at the long
tables with steins of beer before them and most of them
were singing. A surprising number of people, both sexes,
sang with their eyes shut.

They were singing *Zu Augsburg Steht Ein Hohes Haus*
when I entered. I saw Judas at one of the long tables,
singing lustily with the rest. It was a big night for him.

He had a memorable performance behind him and he was surrounded by friends. I did not intrude on him. There was a small table against the wall, a table for two, and I took it. The long tables were the popular ones tonight. My stein of beer came almost instantly and I felt myself a part of the singing in the drinking of it.

They were singing *Ich Bin A Steirerbua* when Judas dropped into the facing chair at my table. There was sweat heavy on his face.

"A man should not drink alone. It is a decadent thing," he said. "My friend Bruno told me you were here."

"You are a busy man tonight. You have a triumph to celebrate. You should be free to enjoy yourself. Friends, not strangers."

"You are my friend," his voice boomed. "I am proud that you are my friend. Did you enjoy the play?"

"Very much. It surprised me in many ways. Your wife told me that you are a great actor. She was right. The two great actors in the play are the Christ and yourself."

A stein had come magically to Judas when he took a place at my table. It was not his first stein of the evening but he treated it as though it were the first. My praise pleased and embarrassed him.

"I like my role," he said. "Strangers will hate me. Some of them, silly folk, will attack me, insult me, leave a room when I come into it."

"Not quite all that."

"Yes. And more. Ask Paul Brockman. He is the Caiphas. Ten years ago he was the Judas. He would never do it again." Judas smiled broadly. "But I like it. I am perhaps an evil man at heart."

"Perhaps not. But a superb actor."

I had him facing me, a friendly man of knowledge

and experience in this strange world of Friedheim, and I could not resist the question that insisted upon being asked.

"Judas," I said. "Forgive me for asking on this night. I have a question. About the play. I described for you that painting of Boniface Rohlmann's which I saw in New York. You said that you knew the scene. You did, of course. It is in the play. How did it get there? It is precisely as Rohlmann painted it and the actors freeze into the scene for a full minute."

"I have given it no thought. He saw the play, this painter."

"Did he? Friedheim staged the play first in 1642. Rohlmann was twenty-three years old, probably not here. That first play would be crude, a small affair, not like this one today. The second play in 1652 would not be much better. He didn't copy from the play. The play copied from him. How?"

The sweat was heavy on the face of Judas. "I must think on it," he said. "Come join my table."

"No. It is your special night."

He rose and slapped my shoulder with a heavy hand. "I cannot think on your problem if you are not there. I must have you with me. My friends will like you."

I walked the long room with him and I was surprised that the people were still singing. We had talked under the singing, or over it, paying no attention to it. The people at Judas's table were singing, too, and some of them were pounding steins. Introductions would be absurd. Judas swept a chair away from an adjoining table and rammed it into a nonexistent space between a man and a woman at his table.

"You know my wife," he said. "You must know her better."

I looked into the mild blue eyes of Mrs. Josef Paskert.
She had been singing until I was thrust upon her. It was
with an effort that I remembered her name. I might think
of her as Mrs. Judas but I could hardly call her that.

"You spoke the truth about your husband," I said. "He
is a magnificent actor."

"He is. He was at his best today but he was nervous
before the beginning."

"Nervous? It is difficult to imagine it."

"Nobody knows that man but me. He is very modest.
This part in the play means very much to him."

"I'm certain that it does. He gives so much to it."

We were talking under the singing, not over it. I
was pleased to have that matter settled. I had not been
sure with Judas. Not everyone sang all of the time. People
smoked or drank or ate some of the delicatessen from the
table platters. A man asked me if I enjoyed the play and
someone else spoke to the wife of Judas. If one had a
place at the table, then one belonged at it. I had a fresh
stein of beer and did not remember when it came to
me nor the number of it. I realized rather vaguely that
I had had several of them. The crowd was singing *Im
Munchen Steht Ein Hofbrauhaus*. It was one that I knew
from long ago and I joined them.

"It is good that you sing our songs," Mrs. Paskert said.

"Even if I sing them badly?"

She laughed but she did not pretend that I sang well.
There was another activity underway. Waiters were serving plates of some indescribable German dish, a mixture
of meats and vegetables and a tawny sauce. It looked
frightful and tasted wonderful. I talked with the wife of
Judas and nothing that we said had any reality. I had
suspended moments during which I doubted that I was

in this place, this town, this country, in the company of these people. There was violin music and, occasionally, someone with a good voice was inspired to solo. The crowd permitted him his spot but there was never any applause. These people knew each other too well.

The wife of Judas turned to me under one solo. "You are interested in the painter, Rohlmann?" she said.

"Very much."

"It is strange that you are interested. My husband will tell you only the facts that belong to him, nothing that is of the priest."

"I know. I have not talked to the priest."

"It would do no good. You are not a Catholic?"

"No."

"A pity. You must think on it. You are a fine young man. It is a terrible thing to be damned."

"I am certain that it must be."

She was such a simple person, so sincere and concerned, so certain in her faith. One had to meet her on her level, respecting her and her belief.

"You must go to the church if you are interested in Rohlmann," she said. "You must look carefully at each of the pictures. One of them will talk to you."

"You mean that there is a Rohlmann painting in the church?"

"That I did not say."

"Thank you. I will visit the church."

She turned to answer some remark of the man on her right. I no longer felt like drinking. The food and the veiled inference to some mystery in the church were enough to take care of the beer that I had drunk. When the wife of Judas turned back to me I asked her the question that I had to ask.

"I do not want to embarrass anyone," I said. "How can I pay for my supper, for the beer?"

She smiled. She was a full-bodied woman with a broad face but she had a soft smile. "It is simple, that," she said. "No one must stay away when his neighbors make the good time, must not stay away because he lacks money. At times we all lack money, *nicht wahr?*"

"That is true."

"That is a great truth. At the end of the table there is a box. On top there is a slit. You can put your money in there. Everyone does the same. One knows what is right, what one can afford. We are honest people. It works out honestly."

"Thank you," I said.

It was a good system, an admirable system. I put in the box enough money for three, or closely as I could estimate, and I hoped that it took care of someone who lacked money. Judas, who was showing the effect of his beers and who had no intention of going home, said good night to me heartily and I made my way through the room to the door. Nearly everyone was singing again and the voices followed me out into the dark night.

There were stars hanging low and a cloud-shielded moon. The crowds were gone and the streets were quiet. There were lights behind the drawn shades and the curtains of homes that I passed and music that flowed out faintly. Some of the families, obviously, had their own private entertainment. The string quartet and the dancers had left the Town Hall fountain. At the Geiger there was light and music but the old man of the fountain, holding his violin reverently, looked down upon a quiet square. A solitary figure sat on the stone rim of the fountain lake. Joan Terrill did not see me until I spoke to her.

"What are you doing out here alone?"

She looked up startled. "It is quiet. I wanted to think."

I could see where the hotel would be noisy. My hotel would be noisy, too. It was not a night for quiet rest, or for thinking. The girl rose slowly.

"I wanted to walk," she said, "but some of these people are boisterous. I was afraid. Are you tired? Do you feel like walking?"

"Walking would be good for me. Where do you want to go."

"Up the hill. I want to see Friedheim shaped like a star."

"You probably can't see the star at night."

"We can try."

Something had happened to her. Something had gone wrong between her and the Beloved Apostle. If walking would help, or climbing, I was a willing companion. Sleep would be elusive, certainly. I had already lost the beer and the drowsiness that comes with it. There was a sense of unreality still, the unreality that I had experienced in the Eisenhut. The moon escaped from the clouds as we walked upgrade and the silver radiance was on the side of all things unreal.

We reached my sketching spot and I looked instinctively for Milky. She was not there, of course. None of the cows, here or elsewhere, was addicted to night life. I waved my hand to the town.

"There it is!"

It was not a star-shaped town tonight. Two of the points were dark and one was hazy. There were two strongly defined triangles that one could identify, if one would, as belonging to a star, but the total effect lacked drama.

"I must see it in the daytime."

"Yes."

She seated herself on a rock, the rock from which I had first observed the star. There was no room beside her. I sat at her feet. It was a strange mood but it was her mood and I left the leading to her.

"I could live in this place," she said. "It is lovelier than any place in which I have ever lived. The people are kind. They are religious. They are good people."

"Yes. They are different, too; different in their backgrounds, their habits, their ways of looking at things, the experiences of their growing up."

"Yes. Yes. You are right. That would explain many things, wouldn't it?"

"I don't know. It depends upon what you wanted to explain."

She was silent, looking down on Friedheim. I thought, as I had thought once before, that beneath the lovely surface, the slanting red roofs and the quaint old gables and the dormer windows, there was much humanity: hatred and envy and jealousy, temper and falsehood and deceit. Beauty never walked alone or stood alone; so much that was not beautiful surrounded it. There were people down there under all the stage setting who were far different than they appeared to be.

"I guess that some women understand men," the girl said surprisingly.

"I thought that all women did, that it started in the cradle with them, that only the male humans were slow."

"No. It is a sex thing, I guess." She had her chin resting on her clenched fist, her elbow on her knee. She was staring into space, speaking to space rather than to me. "Some men have a lot of understanding of women. They frighten me. I am not certain that I understand myself."

"None of us have that certainty."

"Don't you?"

"No."

I knew then that she was wandering along the alcoholic borderline. She had had a little too much of the wine or whatever it was that she had been drinking. She walked and talked, climbed a hill, but she was not thinking or reasoning at her norm. That might not have been the correct explanation, either. Her thinking might have been at her normal level but the inhibitions had been leveled, leaving her bewilderment exposed.

"There is something the matter with me," she said. "I like people, but not close to me. I move away. Sometimes I run. I've known men. I've liked some of them. Some of them have liked me. I don't let anything develop. I didn't at college; not anywhere."

"Why not?"

"I wanted only one ultimate person, one ultimate experience. I was willing to wait. I could not be casual."

The great sense of utter unreality was surrounding me again. I looked up at the girl. She was not looking at me. She was looking toward the town but probably above it rather than at it. Her face seemed white with the moonlight on it and her features were clear, sharply defined. She was a lovely girl.

"An ultimate person stands at the end of a line," I said. "Not at the beginning. You learn what you like along the way, practicing on lesser persons, the ones you call casual. The trick, of course, is not to be derailed by becoming involved with an experience rather than with a person."

She turned her head then. "That is true, isn't it?"

"I don't know. I hope so. I am groping for something. What made you the way you are? Or do you know?"

She looked toward the town again, her chin resting on

the heel of her hand. "I know. Maybe I cannot put it in words. My father is an accountant: steady, reliable, a man concerned for his family. No imagination; none whatever. My mother writes verse. She believes it is poetry. She has imagination of a sort. She does not know that she is always thinking of herself, but she is." The girl shifted position slightly. "That's where I came from. Both of my parents are strictly religious, good people. I have both of them in me, some of each of them, that is."

"You have opened a door," I said, "but only a crack. I cannot see you clearly. Were you an only child?"

"No. I have a brother and a sister. I was never a person to my brother, merely a child. I was close to my sister. We shared things. She was three years older than I. I knew experiences she had, knew about them, I mean. I did not want them for myself, didn't want anything like them. Maybe that explains me, a little."

"It does."

She turned her head. "I shouldn't have told you that, not in the way I did. My sister never did anything really wrong. She just had experiences with boys that scared her. I didn't want to be scared that way; still don't. Maybe I took things too seriously or let them sink in too deep. I don't know. My sister is married now. She is happy. She has two lovely children."

"Don't you want what she has?"

"Sometimes I do. Sometimes not."

"What do you want?"

Her reply was slow in coming. I thought that she was going to ignore the question. When she spoke, she directed her voice to space rather than to me. She did not look at me.

"I want to belong in the world that I live in," she said.

"I do not want to be as other people are, but I want them to accept me for what I am. I know that other people consider me dull and colorless, a square. I've heard them talk. They don't care if I hear them."

"You don't want to be as other people are," I said slowly. "Perhaps that is the key. You disapprove of other people and you expect them to approve of you. Or am I wrong?"

She turned her head and looked at me then. "You are nearly right. Nearly."

Her hands opened and closed, became fists and held tightly to what they became. She was looking at the town again.

"You did not grow up in a strict Roman Catholic family," she said. "I did. There is beauty in it, a very strange security. There is also fear. One grows up with the idea that so many things are sins, venial sins if not mortal sins. One should not sin. One should not share sin with others. As a way of looking at things, it is good, it is admirable, it avoids so much trouble; but not sharing is, as you said, disapproving. One cannot share. One is dancing to a different rhythm. One is trained, one is conditioned, one believes. What can one do?"

There was intensity in her, a desperation of sorts. It was in her face, in her voice, in the gestures of her hands. "I don't know," I said. "Most of us have things that we believe. Most of us live by codes. Maybe we do not think of them in religious terms. We think of decency, of good manners, of honor, of many governing things, the pen names of discipline."

"The pen names of discipline!" She repeated the phrase after me. "I like that."

"It is rhetoric. It doesn't mean anything."

"Perhaps it does.

Once again I had the feeling that this small adventure within a large one was happening to some projection of myself, not to me; that I was not in Friedheim on a starry night, sitting on a hillside with a girl beside me. This girl, if I could believe my experience at all, had spent four years in college and had left her home and her home city for a career. Her career involved working for a cynical, jerk-populated magazine like *Sphere*. It did not seem possible.

"You are disturbed tonight," I said. "Something happened to you. What?"

"Nothing."

She dropped the one word into a pool of silence and I let it sink quietly without any comment. She endured the silence for, perhaps, two minutes then she turned her head.

"What did you think happened?"

"I didn't know. You were doing the town with John the Apostle. You were sitting on a fountain rim when I came along and he was gone."

"He isn't an Apostle. He is a wood carver and a parttime actor. Nothing happened. Nothing at all."

She rose and moved away from the rock. I followed her slowly, not in a hurry to catch up. She reached the narrow path which led down to the village and waited for me.

"You are very patient," she said.

"Wrong. I am more apt to be impatient."

"I don't believe so." She was walking beside me now. "It is an odd thing. I felt that I could trust you from the very first, on the bus when you gave me the best seat. I didn't have the feeling that you were a man at all; you were a friendly person, a dependable person."

"I'd rather be a man if you don't mind."

She made an abrupt gesture. "Of course. I know that. You are, of course. I meant that you weren't playing a man role in my life and I wasn't frightened by you."

"It's a doubtful compliment but I'll accept it."

She walked a few more yards. "I did that badly," she said. "I'm sorry. I would only make it worse if I tried to explain."

She did not have to explain to me. I was a pagan, an unbeliever. Religious people, particularly Catholics, dealt with the likes of us as creatures outside of the lodge, entitled to courtesy and friendliness but not to complete acceptance. The girl lifted her head.

"Why did your wife divorce you?" she asked quietly.

She surprised me with that question, surprised me with the sudden shift from herself to me. "It was quite complicated," I said. "It was something that she felt she had to do."

"Did you agree with her?"

"I did not contest the divorce."

We walked to the edge of the town in silence. It was a quiet town now with no token of revelry by night. The Friedheimers obtained a release for pent emotion within a short span of hours. Tomorrow there would be Mass to attend and strangers arriving, demands of many kinds to be met. The town needed its sleep.

"Divorce must be a sad experience," the girl said. "It does not solve anything."

"No," I said. "But sometimes it is the only refuge for human dignity."

We had reached the Geiger and the girl turned to face me. She did not expect to be kissed and she did not invite any overture. She did not even offer to shake hands.

"I have been a bore," she said. "I have been a bore
and a problem since you first met me on the bus. I am
sorry . . ."

She broke off abruptly, turned, and was gone before I
could say good night.

I stood looking at the vacuum in space where she had
been and wisps of emotion, of conversation, of feeling,
floated in the quiet night. We had been very close to each
other on that hillside, Joan Terrill and I, and we had not
physically touched each other. Her guard had been down
and she had revealed more of herself than she had intended to reveal. She had not been a bore. She was not
dull or colorless or a square. Something that lived deep
in my own being understood her, spoke her language,
found meaning in what she groped to say.

Such thoughts were dangerous to a man. I shook my
head and turned away. "Moonstruck!" I said. "She and
the night and the music! I had better sleep it off."

CHAPTER THREE

My room at the Bahnhof was up under the eaves. There was a table and a chair under the double window, with a flat ceiling over them. My bed was under a steeply slanting ceiling between the window and the door. If that sounds large and impressive, the fault lies in my powers of description. It was a small room.

I came home after leaving Joan Terrill and the hotel was as quiet as the town. I could look out of the window at moonlight in flow across a disorder of slanting red roofs. Beyond the roofs, a reflector of light, was the river. Nobody walked abroad but such ghosts as lingered still in Friedheim, leftovers from a history that had not been forever peaceful.

"Divorce must be a sad experience," the girl had said. "It does not solve anything."

I thought about that, sprawled on the bed, only partly undressed. The moonlight was in the room with me when my head was at bed level, stronger in the room than it had been on the distant river. I could see Joan Terrill as she looked when she uttered her solemn remark about something that she did not, in any degree, understand.

Solemnity was becoming to her as it is not becoming to most people. Her eyes were deep and dark, her mouth soft, her hair a rich, light-catching auburn. She had music in her voice but it was intimate music; her voice would not have been good on a stage. She was, in many respects, immature; or so she seemed to me.

My wife had been a different type of woman, an entirely different type of woman. Her name when I met her was Alicia Weylin and, that, in the end, was how it was again.

I saw Alicia for the first time on October 20, 1965, on the deck of the S.S. *Michelangelo*. There was bright sunlight on the Bay of Naples and our ship was festive with balloons and streamers and waving handkerchiefs. There was music and there were people with tears in their eyes because the sailing of the ship meant good-bye. There was a girl at the rail in a yellow fur and a yellow coat, a dark-haired girl who waved frantically with both hands. I thought, looking at her, that she must be the most beautiful girl in the world.

Everyone milled around the rail until we were well out in the bay. When the girl turned to leave, I braced my shoulders and blocked her. It was very polite but it was still a block.

"I hope that you will pardon me," I said. "I would like to sketch you as you looked when you were waving good-bye at that rail a few minutes ago. You were the only one waving two-handed."

Her eyes swept me and she had not developed that expression in her eyes through listening to someone reading Winnie the Pooh. "I am traveling alone because I wanted to be alone," she said.

"You will be. Nobody is more alone than a girl in a sketch, particularly when she is waving good-bye."

Her eyes still measured me but they had lost their wari-
ness. "You may sketch me," she said, "but you cannot
talk to me."

"I never speak when I'm sketching. If you will please
wait patiently, I will get my gear from my cabin."

"I'll wait," she said, "but not patiently."

She was not on deck when I came back with my easel,
pad and pencils. I waited ten minutes for her. She came
back. She had changed her make-up and she had looked
better before she changed it. That was not a subject for
comment.

"Do you think that you could catch that pose again, the
good-bye and the two hands?"

She looked startled. "Why, of course. Why not?"

She did, too; exactly the same. Her face was wonderfully expressive, her expression combining the joy of leaving, the regret at parting. I worked hard to do her justice
and she did not relax out of the pose until I told her to
do so.

"Thank you," I said. "You must have left someone
behind in Naples who really mattered."

"Why?"

"It was in your face."

She laughed. "I didn't know a soul on that dock. My
friends flew home earlier in the week. None of them wanted
the sea in October."

"But you did."

"I don't know. I never have. Let me see the sketch!"

I showed it to her and it was a good sketch. It caught
the line of her body, the forward thrust of her head, the
two hands waving. She looked at it and drew a deep
breath.

"I had no idea! It's great," she said. "I'll buy it. How much?"

"It's yours. I wasn't trying to sell something."

"Oh!" She stared at me. "I was gauche, wasn't I?"

"The Italians say *goffo*, not gauche."

She was still staring. "I like that."

"Like what?"

"I like the way you handled my question. You didn't say that I was gauche or wasn't. Anyway, I like the picture. I would like to keep it."

"It is yours, all yours. I had my fun in doing it."

She took a few steps away from me and came back. She moved beautifully, with never an awkward turn or careless step. "What table do you have?" she asked.

"Fifteen. I haven't met the other people yet."

"Are you alone? You aren't part of a couple?"

"Half of the answer is yes, half no."

"Let's sit in those deck chairs."

"They aren't ours. You have to arrange for them."

She sat in one of the chairs and waved to the one beside it. "Who is going to arrest us?"

I sat beside her. There was a bit of wind on deck and most of the passengers had gone inside. "I have table five," she said. "It is a table for two and I've already said 'No' to two Italian officers. So, it is still my table. Just me." She gestured with her right hand. "I want you at my table."

She had caught me off guard. "You don't know me," I said. "I could bore you to death."

"No." She shook her head. "I don't want to battle some Italian all the way across the Atlantic. I can handle you."

"You don't know."

She smiled and there was charm in her smile. She had perfect teeth. "Do you want to bet?" she said.

All of Alicia Weylin was there in that first meeting before I even knew her name. I did not see it, of course, but the outline was drawn for me. She could not be any other way than the way she so obviously was. She always revealed herself; in her vanity which verged on conceit, her tricks with her hands and her voice and her eyes, her direct challenging manner of speech, her absolute centering of self, her will to dominance. I saw nothing but a pretty girl, nothing at all.

"My name is Kirk Donner," I said.

"Oh! That's right. I didn't know, did I? It's a nice name. Kirk Donner. My name is Alicia Weylin."

She pronounced the name and waited expectantly. Faint bells rang along my memory band. "It's a show," I said. "You were in a show. I can't pull it out."

"*A Girl Like Emily,*" she said. "We ran a year on Broadway. You didn't see it?"

"I couldn't. I've been away for a couple of years. Europe. Army."

"Oh! The Army."

Her disappointment was obvious. We were not living in an age of heroes. People were not enchanted by uniforms.

"I wasn't a soldier," I said. "Not really. I'll give you a brief biography. I finished four years of college and my draft board was breathing hard on my neck, so I let them have me."

"You could have gone on for a Master's. Everybody does."

"Nearly everybody! I know. Then a Ph.D. After that you teach, whether you want to teach or whether you are any good at it. You are bitter, so all of your students become hippies."

"You *are* a soldier," she said. "You talk like one."

"No. I'm an artist. When the Army discovered that and discovered that I could speak fluent German, I went to Germany. I did sketches for an Army magazine and I sketched a colonel and all of his friends and a general took me away from the colonel. I dreamed up excuses to go to a lot of top museums and I lived a wonderful life. I could have had a commission and a soft career in the Army, but I got out, finagled my discharge in Germany and did a tour of Italy. *Voilà!* I am here."

"It wasn't a brief biography," she said.

"I'm sorry. Tell me about *A Girl Like Emily.*"

She told me. She had a jumpy, digressive, sidetracky way of telling a story but she covered ground. She hadn't had the lead in *A Girl Like Emily.* She had been the ingénue. It was a musical. She only sang two numbers but they were good numbers. She got almost as much publicity as Clover Atley who had the lead. She was telling me about a picture she had made in Hollywood when she suddenly looked at her watch.

"Oh! Dinner! I have to get ready. I haven't unpacked. I will have mail in my stateroom. I know I will have mail." She rose from the deck chair like a puff of smoke. "You arrange with the steward," she said. "My table. Number five. Eight o'clock."

It never occurred to her, and never could occur to her, that the table would be mine as much as hers, a table for two that was occupied by two fellow passengers with equal rights. It was *her* table and I existed at it by reason of her gracious whim. The idea amused me and I had nothing to prove. I merely went along.

She did not appear at eight, of course. It was 8:20
when she made her entrance to the dining room. She was
wearing a sheath-fitting gown of Titian red, red verging
to scarlet, and she was spectacular. She knew how she
must appear to others and she made an entrance, pausing
for a moment as though undecided or uncertain, then
moving to inaudible music, perfectly in step with it. When
she reached the table she let her jaw drop and, somehow,
forced forward her upper row of teeth, so that she looked
utterly idiotic.

"Yuk, yuk, yuk," she said.

I held her chair for her and, for a few seconds after I
faced her across the table, she looked like the village idiot.
Her jaw went back into place then and she smiled at me,
the prettiest girl I ever saw.

"Why the yuk-yuk business," I said.

"I've got a rubber face. I wanted you to see it. And I
wanted those staring biddies at the other table to have
something to talk about besides the red dress. Like it?"

"It's great," I said.

She was a dozen women in one and I began to learn
about actresses. She went light on the wine and she never
touched hard liquor and she never forgot, even when dining
with a man, that she was in the eyes of an audience.
She pulled anecdotes out of the air and she told them
beautifully and she would take a pause in even a very
good story to invite a compliment. I was enchanted by
her and she knew it and, I believe, it amused her.

After dinner we went to a motion picture in the *Michelangelo*'s theater, something called *Circus Days* with John
Wayne and Claudia Cardinale. Alicia referred to Wayne
as "the Duke" and said that he had wanted her in a picture of his when she was in Hollywood.

"Why didn't you go with him?"

"The studio wouldn't let me. They are holding me tight. I've got a picture coming in about a month. Did I tell you?"

"No."

"It is called *The Lady Needed Clothes*. My agent won't let me work for anyone till it comes out, because then my price goes up."

That first day and night was Wednesday. We went to the captain's dinner on Thursday and we discovered that we danced well together. There was an extra something in our dancing; passion probably, certainly an awareness of each other, a sense of build-up, a consciousness of more to come. We did the mad things, too; like piling out on deck at 5 A.M. to see the Rock of Gibraltar. The Rock was invisible, wreathed in fog, but Alicia looked as well in slacks as she did in spectacular clothes. She walked the wet deck as well as she danced.

We learned to like each other very much on the *Michelangelo*. When we landed I had to fly home to St. Louis for a week. We had a terrific reunion when I returned to New York and in three weeks we were married. There was a hotel reception with a lot of show business people and hardly anyone I knew. We skipped a honeymoon trip and moved into a studio apartment that I rented near Gramercy Square. I couldn't afford it but I had a special problem even that early. Alicia was capable of earning far more than I but I could not permit her to support me.

"You are silly," Alicia said. "After my picture is released, money won't matter. They'll be bidding for me. Never mind. Money or no money, I'll love you for a million years."

We knew all about love. Our marriage was a mad, passionate flight into space. Maybe all marriages are, in their beginnings. I do not know about other marriages. As a physical collision between two people, a union of bodies, an ecstatic madness which excluded all others, our marriage was the perfect model for all the marriages to be.

The opening of *The Lady Needed Clothes* was postponed twice and finally set definitely for the sixteenth of November. There were minor irritations for Alicia and her male lead in the picture, Paul Esterling, couldn't come for the première in New York. Neither could the director. I began to feel disaster in the air but Alicia did not seem to feel a thing except impatience.

On the night of the sixteenth, it snowed. The usual camera and crowd stuff outside the theater was brief and the crowd small. Alicia spoke a few words into a microphone and took a bow from the stage, looking marvelous. We settled into our seats and the picture began.

Alicia looked dreadful. The camera was her enemy. It found hard, stiff lines in her face which her mobility of expression normally erased. Her natural charm, the gaiety that she projected, seemed false, bad acting instead of the reality of herself. Within the first two minutes Alicia reached over and gripped my hand hard. Within another two minutes she had abandoned my hand, sitting with clenched fists in her lap.

It was a good story, an amusing picture, and the only thing seriously wrong with it was Alicia. All of the fault did not lie in the camera. Alicia could not resist occasional demonstrations of her rubber face and her yuk-yuk routine, unnecessary to her role and downright embarrassing. We would have left early, slipping out quietly, but she couldn't. She had after-show promotional gimmickry in which she was pledged to participate and she walked through all of that magnificently, carrying triumph in both hands, every inch a star, not letting anyone glimpse her own personal knowledge that she had failed. She showed me what a great actress she could be in those few minutes. It was one of the truly superb performances of her career.

She cried in the chartered limousine of the evening on our way home. In the apartment she exploded. She paced back and forth, throwing her things around and cursing as I had not suspected she could curse. She damned the cameraman and the director and the make-up man. She accused them of giving her hard light and bad angles, of a dozen things too technical for my understanding. The dress that she wore for her première was a Paris original, expensive beyond belief to a man only a short time out of the Army, as I was. She ripped that dress off and walked on it. I could not get through to her with any word of comfort, of encouragement, of love. There was no reaching her.

Our marriage took a new direction, a disastrous direction, from that night; not because of any discord between us but because Alicia had room for only one interest in life; herself.

She had been a star of stars before her picture was released, savoring in advance the triumph that would be hers. She laughed at any hint that we might ever need money and she thought it amusing that I wanted to pay my share of everything if I did not assume the entire expense. She laughed, too, at my feeling of helplessness in her professional life, my concern that I could not help her in any tangible way. She was *She,* destined for big money, bigger and bigger roles, needing nobody. She would not have been like that if the picture were not due to be released, but that picture, to her, was a moon landing already made. It was very, very difficult to come down to earth again.

She became excessively cautious with money except the outlays on herself which she labeled "professional." She pursued directors, producers, all manner of people in a manner that I considered disastrously obvious. She was impatient with me, savagely impatient at times for no reason. At other times she was frightened, defensive, in need of me for reassurance.

"I want to be a great actress, Kirk," she said during one of our calmer intervals. "I want to be the greatest in the world. Please understand that. I won't spare myself. I'll work hard. But I want to be that."

"Greatest at what?" I said. "Comedy? Tragedy? Drawing room?"

"I don't care. I'll do what they ask me to do. Anything."

Again there was a wide gap between us and I could not reach her. She did not really have a goal. She was not compelled by some driving thing within herself to spend her life and her energy and her hope on some particular aim. She merely wanted to be great.

It was impossible, of course, for anyone, even the man who lived with her, to understand an actress. Alicia would emit strange sounds at odd moments, a sort of running-the-scale with nonsense words. She would work for hours before a mirror, with no sense of humor whatever, practicing expressions, eye effects, twists of her mouth and all manner of indescribable gestures and contortions. She would crawl on the floor, solemnly intent, tapping the floor with her fingers, eyes fixed on something that only she could see. She would memorize whole pages of dull books and declaim from memory, just for the practice in memorizing.

It was work, hard work. It was living her thing. She did not exaggerate that. Until I learned better I would intrude occasionally with a remark or a question. Any such break-in would throw her into a rage. She wouldn't tolerate it.

She was not in the least interested in what I was doing or trying to do. Sometimes she went through a brief interlude of seeming interested but it was all surface. She expected me to drop everything at a moment's notice to join her in something that she wanted to do or to play the messenger-boy role. She was the center, the magnetic center, and I had to revolve around her. It was the way her mind worked. She did not know, actually did not know, that she was selfish.

She spent a lot of money on phone calls to Hollywood, to agents and to directors and to all sorts of people. Hollywood was obviously not interested in her after *The Lady Needed Clothes*. Her studio had not renewed its option on her services and her agent was evasive. She was wasting her time and, amateur though I was, I knew that; but I could not tell her. She finally decided that she had to be out there.

"On the ground," she said. "I've got to be on the ground. Phones are no good, Kirk."

We spent our first Christmas together in Beverly Hills, in a hotel that we could not afford. I had planned to take her home to St. Louis as a treat for my family.

I was lost on the West Coast. I could not attend the art showings, talk to art people, or, more important, work. I was a puppet, not an artist, and I could not see where Alicia was serving any purpose in Beverly Hills.

"Why don't you go back on the stage?" I said. "You

are established there. The jabbering pictures aren't worth
a damn any more."

Her lips tightened. "I want another picture."

She wanted, of course, to wipe out a defeat, to prove
that someone else had been responsible for all that went
wrong with *The Lady Needed Clothes*. Someone else was
always responsible for things that went wrong while Alicia
walked invincibly, above all error, above all missteps,
above human weakness and human malice. As her most
easily available scapegoat I knew a great deal about that
side of Alicia's makeup.

Despite her firm denial to me, however, when Alicia's
New York agent phoned to offer her a stage role, she accepted.

The play was similar to *A Girl Like Emily,* a light
musical, and Alicia was the ingénue. The show had been
on tour for three months, heading into New York. Alicia
was substituting for Eva Cowle who was the one weak
spot in the show. That weak spot became immediately the
show's one best asset, the scintillating spot of spots.

Alicia got rave notices on opening night and settled in
for a long run, so happy with the praise she received that
a little of that happiness spilled over on me. It was a
good time. I even settled, after a fashion, into work.

It was during this period that I painted a picture which
I had been carrying in my mind. I titled it formally, "Portal Arch decorated with reliefs; detail." I painted half
of the portal arch of a cathedral, any cathedral, and I
did the inevitable heads which decorated it. The heads
were the heads of prominent authors, actors, actresses,
painters, opera stars, done as the ancients did saints, portraits in stone. It was my first venture into a field that

fascinated me, the doing of a sculptor's job with paint
on canvas.

That one painting earned me an introduction to Ludwig
Lorenson and the beginning of a real friendship. It established friendly contacts, too, with Neil Carlton and Father
Joseph Graney. Alicia, who never understood what I did,
or why I did it, sniffed when she saw it.

"You could have put me in there," she said. "Why in
God's name put Hepburn?"

There was no explaining to her why I could not use her,
nor why Katharine Hepburn stood out as one of the saints
of an actress litany. She could not see that Hepburn
looked wonderful in my pseudostone, like somebody right
out of the Renaissance.

The months rolled over us. Alicia worked in the show
at night and when her performance was over, she needed
time for descent to earth. She liked to go to the late places,
to sit around and talk, to see and be seen. She did not
drink so it was all quite easy for her. Next day she would
sleep till noon. I stayed with her for a while but I had
to see people in the mornings and I had to work. Alicia,
then, was sleeping while I worked and I was sleeping
while she worked. It wasn't the healthiest situation in the
world.

Max Henske came to town. Alicia had known him in
Hollywood and she said that he was a great director. He
was, reputedly, casting for three big pictures in the fall.
"He wants me for the best of them," Alicia said.

"How do you know?"

"He told me so."

I didn't like Henske and I didn't like his effect on
Alicia. She was beginning to make cracks at the stage and

she would throw in occasional sneers at the show in which she was featured. I had not seen the show for a couple of months. When I saw it I was shocked. Alicia wasn't real in it any more. She was doing a lot of rubber face routines and throwing in some yuk-yuks, making low comedy out of what had been light humor. I told her about it and provoked one of the few serious quarrels of our married life.

"You don't know a God-damned thing about show business," she said.

"I know a few things about you. You are an actress, not a clown."

"Yes? Well you wait! I'll show you acting when I get back to Hollywood."

"The screen isn't your medium. The stage is."

"You think so? Well you're wrong." She walked up to me, jabbing my chest with the first two fingers of her right hand. "You can't see past that job they did on me in *The Lady Needed Clothes,* can you? Well, they'll never do that to me again. Never!"

"Who's stopping them? Henske?"

"You're damned right! Henske will stop them if I want him to stop them. Me, I'll do it if I want to do it myself. And lay off the jealousy bit! Max Henske is all right. Max Henske is my friend. And Max Henske is going to put me back on that screen in the fall!"

The Henske complication bothered me. Maybe it was jealousy, maybe not. I didn't believe in him. I was beginning to find myself as a painter and I had been doing some writing about art, but I cut down on my own activity to spend more time with Alicia. Henske went back to Hollywood and everything was fine with us again.

By the time her show closed, Alicia was signed up for a straw hat tour with the revival of her big success, *A Girl Like Emily*. I made part of the tour with her and summer theater was relaxed and was. We made an almost-honeymoon out of it.

Honeymoon, or *A Girl Like Emily*, or whatever you want to name, Alicia never got films out of her mind. Her tour ended at Elitch's Theatre out in Denver, Colorado, and she wired me from there that she was going on to the Coast. She didn't ask me to join her and I was involved in a big showing at Lorenson's; not, unfortunately, my own pictures. I had to let her go and she didn't even write me a letter.

After a month of silence, I wrote to Alicia in care of her agent. I had no idea where she was living, where I could write or phone. Anonymous people sent me clippings from *Variety, Hollywood Reporter,* and other publications which, in the code of their craft, reported the "close friendship" of Max Henske and Alicia Weylin from Broadway. Alicia had always used the Weylin name and it was her stage name so I had no objection to that; I did object to Henske.

Ultimately, when I heard from Alicia, it was a curt note on the stationery of her agent. *We do not have anything together any more,* she wrote. *I want a divorce, Kirk.*

I flew out to Hollywood and I did not have any point of contact with Alicia except the agent's office and there was no cordiality there. They told me that they would report my hotel address to Miss Weylin and that she would call me.

"I'll meet you at your hotel, Kirk," she said when she called. "Six?"

We met at six and the months had done something to her. I do not know if "subtle" is the right word for that something. She looked much as she always had but the hard mask, the rigid something behind the surface of her face, was obvious now without the intrusion of a camera.

"Let's do this decently over a drink," she said.

Decently or not, we sat at a table on the terrace and she said bluntly what she had said in her note. "I want a divorce, Kirk. I don't want alimony or financial settlements, just the divorce."

There was macabre humor in that. I had no money, had never had any, and I was barely making a living. The trip to the Coast had been a major investment for me. Alicia had had some money when I married her and she had probably saved money out of the show and out of her straw hat season. I had never known much about her finances and had never cared.

"You can't get a divorce," I said. "No grounds."

Her eyes were level, cold. "Desertion."

"No. I did not desert you. You deserted me."

"I can get it on desertion."

She was confident and probably justified. Women get what they want from juries and from judges. The cliché was established fact, that men desert women and not the other way around. I played with my liquor glass and I was more than a little sick with the bitterness that moved around in me.

"The trouble with us, Alicia," I said, "is that I am a one-woman man and you are a multi-man woman."

She merely shrugged. "All right. I want a divorce, Kirk."

She had always known how to stay firmly on the

track when she could see where she wanted to go. Deviation from the line of what she wanted was not in her, never in her.

"You can have it, Alicia," I said. "Do it your way."

I came to the end of remembering it in a hotel room in Germany. There was pale light in the sky and it touched gently the soft yellow curtain that hung between my bed and the window. I had not been in that bed all night. I walked the few steps to the window. It was a long time since I had seen a dawn in Germany and the beginning of a dawn lay just beyond the weathered glass.

"Divorce must be a sad experience," Joan Terrill had said. "It does not solve anything."

Speaking now to a memory rather than to another person, I could only repeat what I had said then: "No. But sometimes it is the only refuge for human dignity."

CHAPTER FOUR

The pious people of Friedheim, and the not-so-pious people, and the visitors went to one or another of the various Masses in the morning. It was Sunday morning and the steeple bell rang its summons to each Mass and its solemn accompaniment of the consecration in mid-Mass. The bell intruded on me dimly, registering on my sleeping self and not completely awakening me. At eleven-fifteen I arose and at noon I had breakfast. It was a big breakfast and made lunch unnecessary. The pious and the borderline characters were eating a legitimate lunch when I strolled down the street to the church.

It was quiet inside, with the scent of incense in the air. Sunlight flowed through the stained-glass windows and created patterns on the flooring of the center aisle. There was a high main altar with angels on guard at either end, man-sized angels. Above the altar in one great ascending sweep was a design in bright color and in gold trim, the Ascension of the Lord surrounded by small angels and regarded adoringly by earthbound mortals gazing upward. I had seen many such baroque creations and many that were better done.

It did not matter. The church was quiet and there was
that peace in it that one so often finds in churches, an
atmosphere, perhaps, created by many people praying in it
over a long period of time. I do not know what it is but
I have felt it often and the feeling was strong in this church
of Friedheim. The red sanctuary light twinkled in front
of the main altar and that was a symbol of silence.

There was a painting of Saint Cecilia in the back of the
church, appropriate enough since this was a town of music
and doubly appropriate since she was playing the bass violin
rather than the conventional organ. It was a copy, and a
good one, of Domenichino's painting in the Louvre. On
the right-hand aisle, one third of the way down, there was
a chapel of Saint Crispin and they spelled his name with
a "C" rather than a "K." The statue of the saint was
newer and better done than the one I had seen outdoors,
the one spelled Krispin, but I liked the outdoor one better.

At the end of the aisle there was a confessional and then
a clear space. The stained-glass window, a tepid annunciation scene with an oversupply of flying cherubs, was high
on the wall. Beneath it in solitary, and humble, glory was a
single painting, an old one protected by a sheet of glass.
It was approximately 27"×21" and one had to step close
to it to see it clearly.

It was a Madonna, obviously the Mother of Christ in
intent, and the artist, had scorned such obvious devices as
a halo or a round of glory or a streak of light. She was
walking on a cobbled street. There was a small child on
her left arm and she was steadying him with her right hand.
She was smiling. Behind her, on both sides of the cobbled
street were the houses, wedged close together in rows. They
had symbols on the doors or on outside walls between
windows. It was possible to identify only one of the sym-

bols, the symbol on the door of the house which was to the Lady's right. The symbol was the head of a unicorn. I did not have to see any more. I knew where she was.

The Lady was walking on Kirschbaumstrasse in Friedheim, the street which I had assumed arbitrarily to be the street on which Boniface Rohlmann had lived.

Only then, when I had observed the painting in some small degree, did I read the legend beneath it. There was a framed white card with a text written in the old German script. It read:

> Our Lady of Friedheim. A sixteen-year-old youth of Friedheim painted this study of our Blessed Mother in 1635. It hung in the old church and was lost for a time before it was restored to its present place. The painter, as was his painting, is lost. Pray for him.

I stood there in the quiet of the church and stared at the painting. It was beautifully done. The Lady wore the conventional blue and white robes but the painter had draped them so ingeniously that she might have been wearing the simple peasant dress of her time. There was grace in her walk, lightness, and she was smiling . . . So few of the Madonnas had smiled but this one was a young woman with a small baby and why should she not be happy?

I had done mental arithmetic when I read the message beneath the painting. Sixteen years back from 1635 when this was painted, Boniface Rohlmann was born; in this town, probably on the street where his Lady walked.

This was the painting which the wife of Judas had told me to find. It was a rich discovery, a painting that was worth the viewing in its own right and worth inestimably more to me as the second Rohlmann creation I had seen.

I backed away from it slowly and it faded. It was very
old and it might have been neglected during the lost years
mentioned in the card beneath it. The protecting glass
dimmed it, too.

"I will have to sketch it."

I spoke to the empty church and I spoke regretfully. I
could not sketch the painting in the time that I had. I
would have to wait. Joan Terrill and I had an appointment
at 3 P.M. to interview Anselm Freytag, the actor who
played the role of Jesus Christ in the play. I had grown
easily into the habit of calling Judas by his role name, and
John, but, agnostic though I was, I could not say, or think,
casually that I was about to interview Jesus Christ.

The church was not only a quiet place, it was a friendly
place. There were a great many images of saints, wood
carvings, obviously local products and the more valuable
because of that. There was a magnificent carved crucifix
and that was very old.

If I was unable to imagine myself in the company of
saints, certainly I was in the company of artists.

I knew then, standing in the solemn silence, that there
had been a sound reason behind my avoidance of the Rohlmann subject with Joan Terrill, my reluctance to ask her
for something that, seemingly, I could not obtain without
her. The priest might not reveal any information that he
had to anyone who was not a Catholic, but I was the one
who wanted the information and I was the one to seek it. I
couldn't ask a girl to represent me and I was not certain
that she could do it perfectly if I asked her. I would have to
see this priest myself and either do the job or fail at it.
"Prosit!" I said.

The main part of town was lively with an influx of
tourists, drawn by the play but busy, on a non-play Sun-

day, in sightseeing and souvenir hunting. Joan Terrill was in the office of Rudolf Lobinger, the P.R. man. Mr. Lobinger was still pleased with himself.

"Ah! I was just speaking with Miss Terrill. It is good that I could arrange it, that two American correspondents work together. You shall have the interview with Mr. Freytag together. The other correspondents will see him later. I hope that you are happy."

"I am very happy."

I was going to add that if I were any happier I could not stand it, but there was no sense in being funny. This man was doing his job in his own way and maybe his way was the proper one for the job he had. He disappeared into another room and I turned to Joan Terrill.

"I went to the church," I said.

"Cheers! No novena this time."

"No novena. It is a nice little church."

"Precious! You know, maybe it will seem odd to you, but I feel downright scared of this interview. I don't know what to say."

"Something will come to you."

The door opened and Mr. Lobinger was back. He entered, then stood aside, conveying more or less subtly the spirit and the essence of awe. A young woman moved hesitantly into the room.

"This," Mr. Lobinger said, "is Miss Ursula Dahlen who plays the Blessed Virgin in our Passion Play."

Miss Dahlen was a very ordinary young woman. She was wearing the robes that she wore in the play but no one would ever find in her what Da Vinci, Raphael, Michelangelo, del Sarto, Carreggio, Botticelli, Sassoferrato, and a thousand others had put on canvas. She shook hands with us rather timidly and said that it was pleasant meeting us but that, if we did not mind, she would not be interviewed. She left then and I could only recall her vaguely in the play although she had a leading role. The quicksilver of acting is not in everyone.

The door opened again and Anselm Freytag, the man who played Christ, came into the room. He was wearing a gray suit, a blue shirt, and a gray necktie. He was friendly, not entirely at ease, an impressive man in appearance. In the course of the play, moving from scene to scene, he had suggested many of the concepts of Christ which painters had painted, in person he suggested none of them and yet he wore the conventional Christ image. That is difficult to define or to explain; one felt it.

"I am Anselm Freytag, a maker of violins in this village," the man said. "I have been greatly honored in being chosen to enact the role of our Lord and Saviour. I will answer such questions as I can, but they will be the answers of a country man, a maker of violins, no more than that."

He had carefully prepared that little speech and he won my sympathy with it. People would expect more of him than he could give. Joan Terrill picked up that same thought and made a question of it.

"Do people actually treat you as though you were the Lord? Do they expect blessings and all that?"

He looked at her gravely and in that moment he resembled very closely the Léon Lhermitte Christ of *Supper at Emmaus*. "Yes, unfortunately they do," he said. "I cannot live up to what people expect of me, so I live very quietly and see very few people, during the play."

"But you prepared a long time for the role. You live it intensely. I watched you closely at the press preview. You must feel, at least in moments, that you *are* Jesus Christ. You can't help it."

Joan Terrill surprised me. After her professed fright in facing this interview, she was a confident questioner. She was leaning toward Anselm Freytag, not asking a question so much as professing a belief. He took his time in answering her.

"In the play," he said slowly, "I do the things that the Lord did on earth and I accept the things that he accepted. I speak the words that he spoke. Yes. I do feel that I am the Lord for a short time, acting for him and not myself. It is very difficult to leave the play and come back to my own life. I have to be alone for a time and it is difficult."

Joan's eyes were wide and her face seemed pale. "I'm certain that it must be difficult, incredible, an experience beyond imagination. I don't know how you can face a whole summer of it."

"I am privileged to face it. It is beyond my deserving."

He stared at her for a few seconds, then he smiled faintly and turned to me. I had no question ready. I had been interested in the exchange between himself and the girl. Incongruously, at that moment, I noticed that his eyes were brown.

"My question may not be legitimate," I said. "You are the main figure of the play, the Lord. Your story is a heroic story from the New Testament. The villain of the story is Judas. He betrays you. If he did not do exactly that, there would be no story, no crucifixion, no redemption, no resurrection; nothing. Prophets have foretold it and have foretold the soldiers' gambling for Christ's garments. The soldiers have to do as they do and Judas has to do as he does. *He has to betray you.* So, why, is he a villain?"

The man laughed softly. I remembered how I had liked his laughter in the play, how I had liked the idea of a laughing Christ.

"It is a good question," he said. "We, in Friedheim, discuss such things. The village has lived with this story for centuries. There are ideas about it." He paused and shook his head. "Prophecy sees but does not compel," he said. "I tell you that the bus from Munich will arrive at 5:20 tonight. I am a prophet. It arrives. I had nothing to do with that bus. I do not compel it. It does not have to arrive because I say so."

He smiled and spread his hands. It was a simplicity which obviously satisfied him and I had no right to press him past the answer that he had given to my question.

"One more," I said. "Oberammergau has had trouble with people who say that their Passion Play is anti-Semitic. Do you have difficulty with that question?"

"No difficulty." All the laughter was gone from him now. He had an amazing face, soft in line but firm under the softness. There was in him, I felt, that rare and wonderful combination of strength and gentleness.

"In the play we are all Jews," he said, "with the exception of a few Romans. I, in the privileged role of Jesus Christ, am a Jew and so is the Blessed Mother. So are all the Apostles; all Jews. Judas is a Jew and it is evil of him to act as he does. It is evil of the Jews who cry out 'Crucify him.' What does all that mean? It means that some Jews are good men and some Jews are evil, and, of any people anywhere, we can say the same thing."

He was intensely in earnest, a simple decent man, a maker of violins and a fine actor in a role that he handled with reverence.

"Thank you," I said.

He rose, obviously pleased that the interview was over. He shook hands with us and Rudolf Lobinger went into the other room with him. Joan Terrill and I went back to the street and the tourists and the breathlessness of a hot day.

"I didn't like your questions," she said. "They were unfriendly."

"No."

"I thought so. He was quite wonderful, that man. It would be so easy to believe that you were in the presence of Jesus."

"Even in a gray suit?"

"Yes. Even in a gray suit."

"Well, not to change the subject, I liked your questions. They surprised me."

"Why did they surprise you?"

"You said in advance that you were frightened. You weren't."

"I was. They were questions that I had to ask. I did not see how he could help feeling that he was Jesus Christ when he had to live in such an intense role, but it was a terrifying thing to contemplate."

"Why terrifying?"

"Because Jesus Christ was God."

I did not say anything and she stopped walking. Her fingers gripped my forearm. "You don't believe that, do you?"

"No. I don't."

"How horrible!" She started walking again. "I don't like to think about it. You cut yourself off from so much. There is a great reality. You can feel it if you let yourself feel. You can pray and be aware suddenly that someone is listening."

"That is all lovely. I respect it. It is, I imagine, that mysterious something called Faith. I haven't got it."

We had reached her hotel and she faced me for a moment. "I have to write my story now, the story of the interview. Do you mind if I quote his answer on anti-Semitism?"

"Of course not. It isn't mine."

"You inspired it. Well, all right. Thank you."

She left me abruptly and I thought that she had a genius for that, for swift break-offs that could almost be termed disappearances. I had a story to write myself, an account of many things to be sent to Neil Carlton but I wasn't ready for it. I walked instead to the church and beyond it, to the old streets and to the short street with the long name, Kirschbaumstrasse.

I stood where Boniface Rohlmann had set his easel, in the spot where he must have set it, considering his perspective. I could see where his Lady had walked. The cobblestones were still there and the houses stretched in two facing rows, very old houses, picturesque because they belonged in another century and stood firmly in this one. I looked off to the Lady's right. The house that had borne the sign of the unicorn was no longer there, if it had ever been there. It could, of course, have been the creation of an artist. The house that stood in that spot now was entirely different, taller by a story.

I walked to the house and looked at the door. There was a symbol on it, as on the other doors in the street. It was a simple, obvious symbol, a bass viol, and it belonged to a much later age than that of Boniface Rohlmann. On close inspection, so did the house belong to a later age. The house of his painting was gone. I still liked the house of the Jester but that was in the opposite row and the figure of the Lady had hidden it.

Standing once more where the Rohlmann easel had rested, I stared at the street, finding it all, save the one house, as it must have been in 1635. Sixteen thirty-five! That was three years after the Black Death swept through the town. Three years! And a sixteen-year-old. youth had painted a memorable picture in this spot.

Another date rang vaguely in my brain. Judas had given it to me casually, had tossed it off. We had been drinking beer and I had only half registered what he said: "In the history of Friedheim, only one witch was burned to death . . . Her name was Frieda Neuhardt."

He had given me a date but I could not be certain if the date which floated now in my mind was the date that he had given me or a fantasy of the afternoon. I did not believe that it was a fantasy.

"How could I have missed it?" I said.

It was Sunday afternoon and I did not know where Judas lived. I had to speak to him if only for a minute or two. It seemed doubtful that he would be at the Eisenhut. One would not expect to find him there when the sun was shining out-of-doors, but it was the only address that I had for him.

The Eisenhut was quiet despite the tourist inflow which one could feel all over the town. There were a few people at tables, only a few. It was too early. A large round table at the end of the room had every space of the circumference occupied by men in serious conversation. The table was placed under a rectangular window that was brightly colored in imitation of stained glass. The glass had a picture design worked into it: three small folklore figures, old men in cone-peaked hats who were struggling to move a keg that was, seemingly, too heavy for them. It was an amusing scene and I did not recall seeing it before, but the scene that mattered was the one under the window.

The men at the table were bearded men with the look of Apostles, probably men from the cast of the play. If the Christ had been there in the central spot, it would have done well as a modern dress version of the Da Vinci *Last Supper*. Judas was one of the men at the table but I did not want to intrude on him. I did not want a beer, either, but I went to our usual table, mainly because it was an inconspicuous spot. I did not believe that Judas would see me but he did. He crossed the room and dropped heavily into the chair across from me.

"We are discussing a matter," he said, "perhaps not very important but important to us. I cannot stay out of the discussion except briefly. Can I do something for you?"

"Yes. You told me that only one witch was burned in Friedheim. The year please."

"Sixteen sixty-one. March 24."

"Thank you. May I ask another question?"

"Yes."

"This lad, John. How do you explain him?"

He looked away, shrugged slightly. "An attractive boy. Gifted. From a good family. He is a skilled carver of wood. A good actor."

"That is fine. The person inside of all that is a man. What about *him?*"

The eyes of Judas met mine. "It is a matter that does not concern you."

"It might. I do not ask questions idly."

"Nor do I answer them carelessly. We are well met. There is occasionally here, probably in other places also, a child in an adult body. His body has grown but he has not. One guards him without telling him that he is guarded. In this small town that is not difficult. We know our own people. It is good for him to know a girl, a stranger girl. Perhaps he will grow. Does that answer you?"

"Partly. It is an honest answer. Your concern for him does not include the girl?"

Judas leaned toward me, a study in suspended motion. He was a man with fine eyes, heavy features, a healthy beard that was, probably to keep appearance in his villainous role, untidily trimmed.

"Has there been trouble?" he said.

"No. Don't concern yourself. I will take care of the situation. I had to know what you knew, or thought."

"I know little about anything." Judas rose. "If I can help you, call on me. Leave a message with my wife at the office." He smiled. "To play in this play is like entering a monastery. One retires from the world. I am very happy that I have known you."

He did not wait for any response from me. He gestured awkwardly as he turned away. I watched him walk across the room and join the big table, then I left. The little brown-clad men in the brightly colored window were still struggling valiantly with their jug.

The sky was light out of doors. It was, for some reason, the most fragrant hour of the day. The birds were exchanging greetings or saying good night, a variety of birds with a wide range of voices. I could hear them from all points of the compass. I stood with the stone wall of the Eisenhut at my back and looked at the onion-shaped tower of the church.

On March 24, 1661, Friedheim's only executed witch was burned at the stake. Oddly enough, weirdly enough, that was the date on which Boniface Rohlmann burned, allegedly in Trier.

I could hear the voice of Ludwig Lorenson in my mind. "Trier? I think not. But have it as you please."

Ludwig had known more about Boniface Rohlmann than he had been prepared to admit. He had obviously known how and when Rohlmann died. It would not be strange to discover that he knew, too, *where* Boniface Rohlmann had died. He had not accepted Trier.

I walked back to my hotel with that thought and I wrote a long report for Neil Carlton in which I did not mention the coincidence of dates. That coincidence was a lead that I planned to follow and I had no idea yet where it would lead me.

This report for Neil was difficult to write. I told him of the play and the town and the personalities, of the interview with the actor who played Jesus and of my friendship with Judas Iscariot. I left Joan out of it and I did not mention John. The narrative, despite my limited writing skill and the simplicity of the characters, had a certain magnificence that I recognized on reading it over. Simplicity in a design, in a person, in a painting, provided that it achieves the near-miracle of remaining simple, is always compelling and sometimes high art. As a personal postscript I wrote a single paragraph.

You said, Neil, that I would have the chance of discovering the meaning of our experience with the painting. You may have been jesting, jesting in part at my agnosticism. I do not know. I do remember one other statement of yours—"You may even unlock those two greatest of all mysteries, Good and Evil." You laughed when you said that and the laughter was, certainly, at what, to you, was my absurd belief. I believed that there were degrees in human conduct, high points and low, but not two opposed forces. I did not believe in

Good and Evil. I am shaken in my unbelief. There is more
in this one small town than I could put in a report, more than
I could put in a painting or a book. It may, of course, be no
more than an atmosphere and it may fade into its proper non-
consequence when I go away from it. One way or another,
as you predicted, I have had a unique experience, the logical
ending of which still eludes me.

I took my report, heavily stamped, to the post office
three blocks away and dropped it in the slot. It was late
and the town was quiet, preparing in slumber for tomorrow's unveiling of its play. The moon was hidden behind a
mass of cloud but there was soft light on the rooftops and
in the streets. I had to pass the Geiger on my return trip
and, as I neared it, I heard the sharp click of heels, the
unmistakable sound of someone, a woman, running.

Joan Terrill turned the corner above the fountain and
ran on a diagonal toward the door of the hotel. I was not
close enough to stop her but she could see me. I stretched
out my hand and she waved it away, still running.

"No," she said. "No!"

She was gone then and another figure turned the corner,
too, the corner that she had turned. It was John and he
must have been wearing soft shoes because he ran without sound. He saw me as she had seen me and he veered
to the left on the far side of the fountain. He was a
portrait in filtered moonlight for a hesitant moment and
then he vanished.

The town was quiet again and I walked to my own
hotel without seeing anyone. There had been an incident
and I could not explain it but then, of course, I was not
called upon for an explanation.

CHAPTER FIVE

There was motion, the scraping of feet, the sound of voices, in the street before the full dawn on Monday. The neighborhood birds, accustomed to starting the day, protested noisily against this foreign racket. The racket, however, persisted. A great many of the tourists who had descended upon Friedheim on Sunday were going to the six o'clock Mass which would open the Passion Play season. I rolled over in my bed and let them go.

It was still unearthly early when I reached the dining room but only a few stragglers were left at the tables. The rest were, presumably, already at the auditorium or on their way. Before I reached my table, Joan Terrill came in. Her face was bright with excitement and she was waving a slip of paper.

"Cable," she said. "*Sphere* is all agog, congratulating me on getting the Donner sketches. They know you!"

I reached for the cable. The editors at *Sphere* knew me but they had never been excited about the knowing. The cable, however, was warm and it costs money to put warmth into a cablegram. I appreciated it.

"Very nice," I said. "Have breakfast with me."

"Can't. I had breakfast. I'll take coffee, though."

"The coffee is vile as a rule."

"I know. I can't do anything about it so I drink it. I was happy about the cable. I hope that they pay you a big price for the sketches."

"If they do, I'll buy a white-tablecloth dinner, with wine."

It was pleasant to have her sitting across from me at the table, looking vital, when I was only half awake. She provided contrast with which to start the day. There was nothing in her appearance or her attitude to suggest that she had been running home in a panic in the late hours of last night. Whatever had happened to her, or nearly happened, was evidently over.

"I am going home tomorrow," she said.

"No! I thought that you would be staying longer than I. I am leaving Wednesday."

"I will hate leaving." She looked away and there was a shadow in her face. She had been involved in Friedheim far beyond any involvement of mine. Her shoulders moved in a half shrug and her eyes came back to me. "I fly out of Munich to London tomorrow afternoon. I have one day there, then New York."

It did not have any reality, this talk of Munich and London tomorrow, New York on Thursday; not in our Tyrolean dining room with a church bell sounding outside for the beginning of the Passion Play. She would only be one day ahead of me in the annihilation of distance but a few blocks from where we sat, a company of small-town Germans were moving back two thousand years, moving back solemnly and seriously, creating a semire-ality of their own.

"Have dinner with me tonight," I said.

She nodded her head. "Thank you. I hoped that you would ask me."

Seven thirty?"

"Fine."

She left me on that and I watched her go, more than a little baffled by the whole idea of her. She had certainly changed in her few days as Miss Sphere in Friedheim. It seemed preposterous to say that she had matured, but that was the impression that she created with me. Friedheim, was, undoubtedly, the big adventure of her life. Before Friedheim she seemed to have been relatively untouched in spite of college and *Sphere* and living out on her own in New York; all in the sinful seventies, the decade of the gay and the nude.

I took my portable easel, and the sketch box that belonged with it, and I followed a zigzag route to the church, a route that took me through the street of the violin makers and the street of the cobblers and the short street with the long name on which Boniface Rohlmann's Madonna had walked. Joan Terrill would have probably stopped to fill notebooks with notes on the making of shoes and the making of stringed instruments, but I did not learn a thing about them. The temperament of a journalist was not in me. I did not learn about things which did not interest me and I probably saw only a small part of the fascinating world in which I lived.

The violin makers and the cobblers had been hard at work, unaffected by the Passion Play which had drawn so many people into the auditorium. There were other people working, too, in hotels and shops and on the streets of town. The church was empty and filled with an awesome hush. I walked down the aisle and I was depressed by the multitude of angels, above the altar, below the stained-glass windows, above the confessionals, below the pulpit. There were the saints, too, a great many saints. There was humanity in them, that strange sense of human warmth that even a mediocre artist seems to evoke from aged and seasoned wood.

My approach to Boniface Rohlmann's Madonna was slow, deliberate, carefully timed. I met her for this second time head-on, walking into her street from the opposite direction. She walked with grace and she smiled and she held her child with a gentle reverence. She was a lovely woman with the joy of life in her and Friedheim, only perhaps because the artist had given it to her, was her town.

I set up my easel with the board on which I proposed to work. I was going to copy with pencil what this man had done in oil and I was going to make some color notations, too, for the painting that I would attempt when I got home.

Work to me is a concentration, a blotting out. If I can leave my own life and move into other lives, I work happily, seeing them on their terms rather than on my own. There are artists who dominate their work, placing each pebble precisely in place, arranging the set of a drape, the shape of a flower; making each object a unit in his, the artist's, design. I cannot do that. Concentration carries me into other lives, into another environment, and I paint what I find there; arranging it not at all.

The canvas on the wall took me to Kirschbaumstrasse. The houses huddled together and I could see the unicorn clearly on the nearest door. The street was cobbled, uneven, but the Lady walked on it confidently. Her expression, the light in her eyes, said that she was happy to be where she was, proud to be where she was. A boy had painted this picture before me, a boy who had genius in him, and he had given to his Madonna the happiness and the pride that was his own. His Madonna had outlived him and now she no longer reflected an artist; the street was hers, and the town was hers, and the fascinated eye of the beholder.

Detail by detail the painting floated from the wall to the board on my easel, dividing itself yet remaining in its frame undivided. I did not hear the man come in but I became aware of him ultimately without turning my head. He was sitting behind me in a pew. My awareness of him seemed, somehow, to register on him and he spoke.

"You need more light," he said. "I shall bring a candle."

"Thank you."

He shuffled off and in a few minutes he was back. There was electricity in the church but obviously not within easy reach of the spot in which I sketched. The man behind me placed a tall main-altar candle, hesitated momentarily, moved the candle, moved it again, then planted it firmly. He had a good eye. The light touched the picture and brought life to it. It had been alive before but mainly as a projection of my own interest, a reflection of my own imagination. It took on an added dimension with light and because the light was from a candle flame, there was new motion in the painting, the sense of breeze, the very real sense of a woman walking.

The man who had brought the candle was, as I suspected, the parish priest. He was a short, thin man in a black cassock; in his sixties but straight and, despite a lack of weight, a strong man. He had come from the soil, or his parents had. His features suggested a modeling in clay rather than sculpturing in bronze. He had a straight nose which was a trifle long, a firm mouth with a lower lip that protruded slightly, a thrusting chin, deep wrinkles

in his forehead. In the nose-mouth area he had brown
liver spots. His hair was thin and straggly, black turning
gray. His eyebrows were untidy.

"The light was not good. Not bright," he said.

His English was halting so I replied to him in German.
"I am grateful for the candle. It brings out detail that
I would not want to miss."

He nodded. He seemed visibly relieved that I spoke
German. He was courteous but I did not feel friendliness
in him. I was not one of his people in faith and, perhaps,
he crossed that line with difficulty.

"You like the painting?" he said.

"Very much. The painter did not create a Madonna who
looked like an overdressed doll. He painted a woman."

The priest looked thoughtfully at the painting. It was,
conceivably, a point which no one else had ever raised.
"That was, perhaps, a fault in him," he said.

"How?"

"The Blessed Mother to the Church, to the faithful, is
a legend of the spirit. We have the Immaculate Concep-
tion, the Annunciation, the miraculous nativity, the As-
sumption. We are not, in these chapters, dealing with a
mere woman. All of this is in the supernatural. Such things
do not happen to an ordinary woman and there were
great painters who understood this. The painter of that
picture was young. He lacked understanding."

"I prefer this painter. He painted his Lady walking on
your streets."

"A fancy. Not a reality. She never walked on them."

"Are you certain of that?"

I was feeling a kinship with this priest despite the faint
hostility that I felt in him, a kinship, perhaps, of those who
are opposed, a walking on common ground. I had to

discover through him the existent facts about Boniface
Rohlmann and, reputedly, he released his hoarded facts
only to Catholics. He pondered my question now, his eyes
fixed upon my face.

"I do not understand the point you are making," he
said slowly. "The painter indulged a fancy. The result is
something lovely. It is, to some people, a poetic fancy.
It is not fact. He should dress poetry in the garments of
poetry and not in the garments of fact. It is inconsistent
of him."

"You disappoint me." I picked up my pencil again.
"I have seen your play. If I believed as you believe, if
I could accept that play as fact, I would believe that the
Lady walked on the streets of Friedheim."

I turned back to my work. The man behind me was
silent, probably out of consideration, out of respect for
what I was doing; perhaps because he needed time to
think of what I had said. The hands of the Lady were
the hands of a German country woman of 1635. What
else could they be? They were broad hands with short
fingers but there was beauty in them. I took another pause
period. The priest had been awaiting that pause.

"I did not disapprove the work of this artist," he said.
"I merely questioned it through another artist. His painting was packed away, carefully packed but still away, until
I became pastor. I framed it and placed it where it is.
I wrote the little message beneath it." He paused and
made a deprecatory gesture with his right hand. "I am not
of Friedheim, not the heir to its tradition. I am of Lands-
berg, a much different town and yet much the same."

"All towns are the same if you probe deeply enough,
if you get down to the people. I am Kirk Donner."

"I am Father Albrecht Schecker."

He did not offer to shake hands but he was definitely not unfriendly now. I was sitting in one pew and he in another during my break.

"Boniface Rohlmann was a great painter," I said. "One of the truly great, despite the small evidence that we have, the few paintings."

The priest had straightened when I mentioned the Rohlmann name. He sat very straight. "What do you know of this?" he said. "Who has named the painter of this picture to you?"

"No one. It is obvious. He was born here in Friedheim in 1619. Your message beneath the painting states that the painter was sixteen in 1635. How many painters, young or old, has Friedheim had?"

"The name Rohlmann! Where did you learn it?"

"I saw a painting of his in New York, a tremendous painting. It interested me in the man."

It would have been an experience to study Father Schecker's face at that moment but I turned back to my work, deliberately casual. He sat quietly in the pew, respecting that work of mine. We were alone in the church and, in effect, we were alone in the town. People were watching the trial of Jesus.

The painting was a simple one, a single figure and two rows of houses, but, like most truly simple things, it had its depths, its points of significance that were suggested but never hammered home. The houses were without signs of life but there were symbols on the doors and on the spaces between windows. One could see the symbols as present but could read only one, the sign of the unicorn. I had finished the Lady and the houses were roughly drawn. I turned again to the priest.

"What is this picture in New York?" he said. "Where is it?"

"I will make an exchange with you, Father. I will describe the painting if you will tell me what you know of Boniface Rohlmann."

"I know little. It would matter little to you. There is no point."

"I will judge that. You see, I have some knowledge of Rohlmann myself."

His eyes narrowed. "You are a stranger. How can I know that you have seen this painting that you mentioned?"

This was the crucial moment. I could lose him by overshooting or undershooting. The caution of a German countryman could turn swiftly from caution to suspicion, from suspicion to antagonism.

"The painting had magic in it," I said quietly, "genuine magic. It could not be exhibited."

The fact had not been apparent that the priest was holding his breath but I heard the breath sigh softly as he released it.

"What is it that you wanted to know?" he said.

"His death. Allegedly he died in Trier on March 24, 1661. I don't believe that he died there. An alleged witch, Frieda Neuhardt, was burned to death in Friedheim on that date. Was that name false? Did Rohlmann die here under a woman's name?"

The face of Father Albrecht Schrecker was a strong, firm mask. It would not have been out of place on the portal of any cathedral. He could have evaded my question because I had not worded it well. He did not choose to evade.

"I know nothing of his death," he said. "The parish record states that two condemned people were burned to death on the date that you mention. The record reads: 'Frieda Neuhardt, witch, and companion.' The companion is not named."

"But you believe that the companion was Rohlmann, don't you?"

"I have no reason to believe or to disbelieve. I do not know."

"This town could burn one of its sons," I said bluntly, "then conceal his identity because he was a son of Friedheim."

"That is possible. It is long ago. He might have had close family living in the town. The burning was terrible. People might have tried to save the family as much as possible. We cannot know the situation, so we cannot judge. England burned sorcerers and witches. So did France. Thousands of them. Friedheim burned only the two. There is none other of record."

"I don't believe in sorcerers or witches or the burning of people to death. It is all superstition, cruel superstition."

"No. You are wrong."

"What about the trial record? What did they do, these two people?"

"The record has not survived."

"What else can you tell me of Boniface Rohlmann?"

"Little. He was born here in 1619. Baptised July 11th of that year. There was one Rohlmann among the plague victims of 1632: Karl Rohlmann. The family probably moved away from Friedheim. The church record, you know, is of births and marriages and deaths; not of moving out of the town."

"You were interested, yourself, as I am, in the Rohlmann history?"

"No. I was interested in the boy who, at sixteen, painted that picture. It has purity in it."

His eyes challenged me and I did not rise to the challenge. I did not know if the painting had purity in it or not. It was an interesting point.

"I have told you what I know," the priest said. "Now tell me of that painting in New York."

He sat back in the pew and folded his arms. He had gone as far as he intended to go and he was ready to weigh my story with suspicion. I told him of the invitation to view the painting and of the people who were present. He interrupted to ask about the priest, surprised obviously that a priest was present.

"Father Graney is a knowledgeable man in art," I said. "A Jesuit."

"Ahhh!"

That seemed to explain everything. He was not surprised at the presence of a Jesuit in what, to him, was odd company. I worked into the painting slowly, describing the effect of witnessing the scene, of occupying a vantage point just off the action. His features tightened when I described the scene.

"You saw that yesterday," he said. "It is in our play, exactly as you describe it."

"Yes. That is something that I would like to have explained to me. It is a unique scene. You do not find it in other paintings. You will find the scene preceding it and the scene following it; not this scene. Yet it is in your play."

"In its proper place, in the sequence."

"Yes. And with the pause, the completely arrested motion, that you give to other paintings; to the *Last Supper, The Agony in the Garden,* the *Descent from the Cross.*

It would be too easy to say that Rohlmann saw the scene in the play and copied it."

"Why too easy?"

He did not have to ask that question. He knew the answer. I replied without indulging in byplay. "There were only two Friedheim Passion Plays during the time he lived, 1642 and 1652. They would have been simple, primitive affairs, nothing like the play of today, and he was probably not in Friedheim for either of them. He painted in Bamberg and Würzburg, and he, unquestionably, studied in Italy."

The priest made no comment. His face was blank except for the interest in his eyes. "There is another explanation," I said, "and it has to be the only explanation."

"I would like to hear it."

"Boniface Rohlmann painted that picture that I saw and he undoubtedly knew that it was his great achievement. He brought it home to Friedheim and someone here, who was working to expand the play, saw it and either sketched it or wrote a description; then Rohlmann and the painting were in trouble and fled to Würzburg. Some Jewish people there hid the painting. It came from there to New York."

"Trouble? What do you mean by trouble?"

"I told you that there was some magic in it, in the painting, something inexplicable."

It was my climax and I made the most of it, explaining, scene by scene and person by person, the showing of the painting. I even included Robert, after a half resolve to leave him out. The priest heard me through in silence and when I finished my narrative he rose to his feet and walked down to the altar rail of his church. He stood there for several minutes facing the altar, his back to me; then he walked back.

"You say that you do not believe in sorcerers or in witches," he said hoarsely, "but you believe in this painting that you describe to me, in the magic of it."

"I cannot help myself. I saw it."

"And you did not see the witches or the sorcerers although the people who did see them have written about them. To you the testimony that they offered was superstition."

"Yes. I am afraid that it is still mere superstition."

"And you may be right." The priest sat down heavily in the pew. "I cannot prove you wrong. But consider. Before Christians came, this country belonged to the pagans. They had many gods. I do not know if their gods were angels or devils. Probably both. People prayed to them and made sacrifices. Small cults still believe in those gods. There are strange things. You have heard of vampires and werewolves. They are not mere horror stories. People here, many people, will tell you tales of them. There is a long tradition."

"I don't doubt that. You are a priest and an intelligent man. Do you believe in them?"

His face was wet with sweat and he was obviously embarrassed that he had talked so much. He made a brushing gesture.

"Intelligence. Thank you. The Church appreciates that in a priest but does not demand it." He laughed. "You will discover that. You ask me what I believe. I will tell you. We have talked of magic in painting. I will tell you what you probably know without my telling."

He paused and he was not looking at me. He was looking at Rohlmann's Madonna. "There is magic in pictures, magic painted into them, that is white magic, serving God. There are several Madonnas in Europe that have been known to weep, observed by many people with tears running from their eyes. The paintings have been examined by experts who found no trickery, nor trace of trickery. There are paintings of saints where the saint has bled. There are at least two Madonnas in paintings whose eyes have come to life and moved on occasion. I have seen none of this but I believe in the men who investigated."

"Interesting. Have you heard of any painting such as I described?"

"No. As you described it, it sounds benevolent, working no evil, perhaps pointing a lesson to the observer. It could be white magic; perhaps not. The only paintings like it of which I heard are evil paintings."

"How evil?"

"Again, I have heard, not seen. There are cults which own paintings that, seemingly, have life. There are paintings of demons which answer questions, yes or no; not speech but the movements of lips. The lips move when a question is asked."

"Do you believe that?"

"There is always the possibility that the fact reported is actually fact if the reporter is a person of integrity. I have heard, too, of demons in paintings who bleed as the saints in paintings bleed."

He was a sincere man. He had, beyond doubt, been exposed to many country stories and legends through most of his life. He had been fascinated by the occult while remaining at a reasonable priest's arm length away from it. If he believed what I could not believe, I had to respect his right to believe it.

"To me," I said slowly, "there is no absolute good or absolute evil. People shape their lives according to what they want or what they believe or what they are taught. They stumble along, scoring triumphs or suffering defeats and they pick up habits, some of which destroy them."

The priest shook his head. "The truth is in our Passion Play. It was in that painting of Boniface Rohlmann which you described to me. Do you know the key word?"

"Probably not."

"Guilt."

He waited, watching me, and I knew that I had walked into one of the most ancient of traps. I was engaged in debate with a priest on the priest's own ground.

"Consider the Passion Play," he said. "You can say that Judas is a guilty man for betraying Christ, that the priests were guilty for deceiving him and concealing the fact that Jesus was to be killed. You can say that Pilate was guilty in condemning Jesus while considering him innocent and that the crowd was guilty for demanding that Jesus be crucified. You would be correct. They are all guilty but each man has to face his own guilt alone, neither comparing it to the guilt of another man nor excusing it. Your viewers of the painting could not do that. Man will not look at his own guilt."

"I did. I despised what I saw myself doing in the painting but it disturbed me less than it disturbed my fellow viewers."

"You were doing what in the painting?"

"I was stooping to pick up a rock. I was going to throw that rock from a sheltered position in the crowd."

The priest nodded. "You are an atheist?"

"No. I am an agnostic."

"Jesus was not God to you."

"No."

"You saw yourself about to throw a rock at a man. Your companions saw themselves committing offenses against God."

I was about to object, to point out the fact that Ludwig Lorenson had not seen Jesus as God any more than I had; then I remembered. Ludwig had not been disturbed by any action of his that was directed at the lonely figure in the middle of the clearing. Ludwig had seen himself as the stalwart Roman soldier who was thrusting people out of his way. Ludwig saw his offense as an offense against the people.

"There is Good and there is Evil," the priest said. "There are people who bring beauty into the world and people who destroy it; people who heal hurts and people who cause them; people who teach and people who distract; people who pray and people who curse." He made a gesture of helplessness. "The subject is vast but this is true. There are mediocre people who do not know what they serve and there are those who deliberately serve Evil for some advantage that they see in it. There are, too, those who choose to serve Good."

"Also for an advantage that they see in it."

"A little of that, perhaps, in some of them. Only a little. Good promises no temporal advantages. The rewards come, often unexpectedly, out of the acts themselves. Those who serve Evil demand tangible advantages. As Faust did."

"Faust was a legend, a story, not an actual person."

"Perhaps. Perhaps not. No matter. He was a symbol, a true symbol."

"Of what?"

"Of man tempted by the seeming rewards of Evil."

"You've lost me," I said. "The rewards of Evil, even as you put it, are not 'seeming'; they are real. Men profit from Evil and, as you say, the decision is their own."

The priest sat quietly. He was a very homely man, an insignificant man. One would never, reasonably, expect profundity from one who looked as he did.

"No believer in immortality serves Evil deliberately, as a matter of decision," he said quietly. "That is the final test. Believers in one life, no hereafter, do not fear Evil and if Evil offers rewards they are tempted."

"I know many men who do not believe in immortality and who serve no evil," I said. "Fine decent men who do all your good things: bring beauty, heal hurts, teach."

"Yes." He smiled faintly. "Put that way, it is like attempting to fix guilt. In the end, a man stands alone, measured by his own deeds. If he does not believe in immortality, immortality may believe in him."

The priest rose to leave, drawing his cassock about him. I had an impulse then and I did not stop to weigh or to measure it.

"That Madonna of Rohlmann's meant much to you or you would not have placed it here. I would like you to have, personally, the copy I have just made as a memento of this time that we have spent together."

He stood motionless, like something carved from wood as were the images in his church. "I could not. You did not do it for me. I could not repay you in any manner."

"I may have done it for you without knowing that I was doing it. I have had payment enough."

I took the board on which I had made my sketch and handed it to him. He looked at it and when he raised his eyes to mine there was moisture in them.

"You will make another?" he said. "For yourself?"

"Yes. This afternoon."

"You are an agnostic, you say. I do not know. You are a sinner. I have no doubt of that. I have never met a man who was not." He looked again at my sketch. "This is a great gift. I shall remember you."

He raised his right hand, made the Sign of the Cross and turned away. I wasted no time in analyses, in wondering why I had given him the sketch. It was lunchtime and I went to my lunch, putting him out of my mind.

When I returned to the church there was a fresh candle in place before the Madonna of Friedheim. I lighted it and I went to work. People entered the church, prayed, and left in the course of the afternoon, many people perhaps. I paid no attention to them and they did not disturb me. When the second sketch was finished I held it to the light and studied it. The Lady of Friedheim walked happily on the humblest street in town and, even in my copy, she was a lovely person. It was not a bad copy. To my eye it was much superior to the first sketch that I made, the one that I had given to the priest. I had not believed that it would be.

"All of which proves something or another," I thought, "or proves nothing at all."

I started back to my hotel, astonished to discover that there had been a heavy rain. The footpaths were wet but the sky was clearing. There was no one to whom I could speak but I imagined myself saying:

"I did not know that it rained. I knew nothing about it. I was in church."

The idea amused me and that, of course, may prove that I have a childish mind.

CHAPTER SIX

There was a note for me at my hotel. It bore neither greeting nor salutation: no "Dear Anything." *I am still accepting your invitation and allowing you to take me to dinner,* it read, *but I have reserved a table here at my hotel. I hope that you will not mind tolerating a feminine impulse. Joan Terrill.*

She had obviously signed it *Joan* originally, then added the Terrill. The *Terrill* was so patently added, not in the rhythm of the rest of the note. The jugglery amused me and I needed to be amused. The afternoon's work had been demanding and the talk with the priest had been challenging. Climaxing it all, I had had to stand in line for my turn at the shower, down the hall from my room.

Joan Terrill was waiting in the lobby for me when I reached her hotel. She was wearing a dark blue dress which I had not seen before and a carelessly tied light blue scarf. One would not expect the contrasting blues to emphasize the deep auburn in her hair, but they did. She had reserved the booth off the main dining room in which I had seen her with John. It was a snug booth, one of three against the west wall, with a pseudo-lion head at the peak of its pseudo-stone arch. One had a measure of privacy in one of these booths and one was less a member in a mob.

"What are you trying to do?" I said. "Exorcise something? Lay a ghost?"

"Maybe I am. You should not notice."

"Why not?"

"Because there are some areas that are peculiarly feminine. A woman feels safe in them and discerning men pretend that they do not know about them."

"Discerning men may have done that once. May have! In Victorian times, or Edwardian. Not any more."

Her eyes were steady. "There are still men with decent reticences. You are, or could be, one of them. Never mind. Shall we look at the menu."

We looked at the menu. I was beginning to understand how she had survived in a world of crudely motivated people, in college and on *Sphere* and elsewhere. She commanded her feminine areas. She had learned how to stop any would-be intruder at the boundary line. She must have made herself fantastically disliked in many groups, many communities.

We ordered veal and, although the textbooks have doubts and reservations about it, we had white wine. I lifted my glass to her.

"You are going home," I said. "To the next assignment, whatever it may be!"

She touched my glass solemnly with hers. "I shall probably climb back into my rut now, back to the research, the libraries, and the books and the letters to write."

"You did all right with Friedheim, didn't you?"

"I believe so." She waved her hand in a careless gesture. "I am not, however, a girl correspondent type. I know that. Given my choice, I would probably want to be. Never mind! I had a fantastic experience today. I can't get it out of my mind."

"What kind of experience?"

"I went back to the play. You knew that I would. I didn't go for all of it. I skipped much of the early part." She paused a moment, running the tip of her tongue over her lip, her eyes far away from me. "After Jesus was condemned to death, it started to grow dark. The storm built up so fast that it was frightening. Lightning was flashing in the sky when they were nailing him to the cross and the rain broke just as they lifted the crosses into place."

She paused again. "It was exactly as it was that day on Calvary, just as the Gospels described it. I never saw anything like it. I will never see anything like it again. That man on the cross with the rain beating on him!"

"You don't believe that there was anything miraculous about all that, do you?"

She shook her head slowly. "No. I would like to believe so. I don't, really."

"It is the time that storms come in this valley at this season," I said. "They probably have that storm effect at the crucifixion many times. They probably time the play for it."

"I prefer not to believe that." She sipped her wine thoughtfully and looked at me over the rim of the glass. "I am not the only one going home," she said. "How about you? What will you do?"

"I've wondered about that myself. I have pictures that I want to paint. My own choice of subjects, of course, and my own treatment of them. People with checkbooks are more fond of artists who take dictation or who serve causes or who glorify the correct people."

"And you don't do that?"

"I haven't so far."

She looked away into the near distance. She did not try to tell me that I was right, that I would win eventually by sticking to my principles, that an artist placed art above all else. Her mind was too honest to deal in such bromides.

"I believe that you will be happy in whatever you do," she said. "You, too, took something out of Friedheim, something that you have not examined yet."

"I don't know."

The urge to tell her about Boniface Rohlmann was a temptation that I had to resist. I had no starting point. She would not understand the background. I could not explain the background, either, because I did not understand it myself. All of Friedheim, past and present, might be in that story of Rohlmann and his painting if one knew the story in its entirety, but one never knew any human story in its entirety. The shadow areas which hold the seemingly unimportant secrets and reticences become important because they are hiding places, distorting the human story.

"There is one thing that I want before I leave," Joan said. "I want to see this town again from the place where you sketched the cow. I want to see the star shape clear at night."

"It may not be clear. This town goes to bed early and it is Sunday night."

"Can we look?"

"Of course."

We went out to the streets of town and they were lively streets. A great many people who had seen the play were going back to Munich on late buses and other people, who wanted to see the play tomorrow, were arriving. They were German people for the most part, a few Slavs, some French. The languages blended pleasantly as European languages always do in the centers where languages meet.

There were young people congregated at the edge of the circle which surrounded the fountain. They were sitting on the ground, most of them, and there were two guitars. The songs they sang were old German songs, sentimental, tuneful numbers, a far cry from the noise numbers of the hippie cult. Germans, of course, had hippies, too, but Friedheim was off their beat, not a setting that appealed to them.

We stood in the shadows listening, Joan and I, not finding comment necessary. Our mutual decision to stop and listen was, itself, comment. Eventually we moved slowly away and, as we did, a solitary figure moved out of the deeper shadow behind us.

I recognized John as he ran across a broad patch of moonlight north of us. He was wearing a white sleeveless shirt and white trousers and I saw him in profile. There was grace in him and beauty. The silver light rested on him and, in that moment, he resembled the lovely statue of Puck in Washington's Folger Library. I did not, however, think of him as Puck. Two more lines from Elizabeth Barrett Browning moved to their own music in my mind, baffling in their isolation as two lines yet saying, perhaps, all that they had to say:

> Yet half a beast is the great god Pan
> To laugh, as he sits by the river.

I looked at Joan. She was looking straight ahead and if she had seen the Apostle she gave no indication of the fact. When we had covered perhaps thirty or forty yards, she spoke cryptically, her words unlinked to anything that we had seen or done.

"A child in a man's body is frightening," she said. "Incredible. I wouldn't have believed."

She stopped there. I waited for her to continue before I spoke. "How?"

"Never mind. I don't want to think of it."

We were leaving the town behind us. The singing voices had grown faint but we could still hear them, distant rhythm that floated in the quiet night. The moonlight was off to our right, a wide beam of light rather than a flat pattern. We came into my field of the cows and stopped where I had planted my easel.

Friedheim was spread out below us and it was a star, not a clear, clean five-pointed star as it was in daylight but still unmistakable despite the unevenness of the light. That banding of many lights in one area, few in another, produced a blob-like effect, a star that was slightly obese. To Joan, however, the beauty was there, the something that she wanted to see. She stood, silent, looking at the misty picture, light overlaid with moon radiance, then she turned her head.

"I am glad that I came," she said. "Thank you for taking me."

We walked, by mutual consent without vocally deciding, to the flat rock half buried in the earth at the edge of the field. There were four trees, like dark sentinels on our right, and the town lay below us on the left. One could not see the star outline when seated on the rock but there was magic in the whole valley, the small town and the long silver-tinted approach to it.

I was very much aware of the girl, aware of her as I had

not been aware of a woman in a long time. She had one knee locked in her clasped hands. She rocked slightly. Her hair was a dull-red halo.

"Have you ever been lonely?" she said.

"Many times. Often."

"I wonder. People are lonely in different ways. I am certain of that. You have been married. That is a cure for loneliness. I wonder if anyone is ever lonely again in the same way once they have found a cure for it."

"Marriage isn't a cure for it."

"It must be."

"No."

"Maybe divorce changes things. A little anyway. I cannot imagine divorce. It severs people. It shouldn't. Do you ever see your wife? Your ex-wife?"

"She is dead."

"Oh! I didn't know. I would not have brought it up."

"It makes no difference. That severance you were talking about is a very real thing, more real than marriage sometimes. And a marriage has loneliness in it, any marriage. I'm certain of that."

"But not real loneliness."

"Yes. Real loneliness."

She shook her head. "I don't believe that you know. You are an artist. Maybe it is not the exciting life that it is supposed to be, but you know a lot of people, you are admired by a lot of people."

"You are daydreaming. A man sitting in front of a canvas with a brush in his hand is the loneliest man in the world. The antidote for loneliness is sharing. Who can share what goes on in the mind of an artist? Who can share the tracing of lines, the balancing of color, anything he does?"

"You must have lived a strange life," she said.

"No stranger than anyone else. How about you and the way of loneliness? You are an attractive girl. Men would be drawn to you. You work in an exciting office. Why isn't your life too full for loneliness?"

She rocked slowly, looking out over the valley. A large nightbird swooped down past her and vanished into shadow. She paid no attention to him.

"Maybe I am a coward," she said. "Or a misfit. Most of the companionship offered to me is crude or pseudo-sophisticated, a cheap experience rather than a sharing. I could be a part of a person, I believe; of another person, that is. I cannot be just part of an episode. I am putting that badly. A lot of us are lonely because we won't pay the price of not being lonely."

She turned her head as she spoke. Her eyes looked enormous. "I am not a self-pitier," she said. "I am not pitying myself. I would despise that. I am just wondering."

"I know."

I did know. The inarticulate groping! The restlessness that found no outlet! The reaching for something that was not there and that I realized was not there before I reached! The inadequacy of temporary people and the emptiness of self! I knew that whole package, all of it!

The girl seemed to float before my eyes, a creation of the night, of the moonlight, of shared words, of an atmosphere that, probably, the old gods knew before there was a Friedheim. My hands sought her of their own volition and, once they touched her, she was warmth and softness and wonder. She uttered one frightened cry and she struggled weakly, then she ceased to struggle. She submitted limply to the first long kiss and she kissed me as I had kissed her. It was an old madness, always new, and one did not reason with it.

We rolled off the bench and onto the soft grass. She was not resisting me but she looked up into my face and there was fright in her, fright and something else. Her body tensed and my voice came from somewhere, from a long distance away. It spoke to that something else that I sensed, not to her.

"Are you a virgin?" I said.

Her answer was a long time in coming. Her voice had to travel a vast distance as my voice had traveled. It was a faint whisper when it reached me. I was looking into her wide, dark eyes.

"Yes," she said.

I left her. I rose to my feet and I walked away, stumbling. I wanted her more than I had ever wanted anything and I did not know why I stopped. I walked up the hill and there was moon silver in the grass, long shadows under the trees. I stopped walking and the earth seemed to tilt slightly. I was afraid that I was about to be violently sick.

Something inside of me was arguing. Something was telling me that I had gone against nature, that I was a human being with a great need that only another human being could fill. The girl was a human being with the same need. We had both been roused by the something we had shared, the temporary antidote to loneliness. A great aching want had swelled to tide strength and I had stopped it. Why?

I did not try to answer the argument. I had not obeyed any moral code in stopping any more than I had attempted seduction in starting. I was not Little Lord Fauntleroy and I did not believe in the gestures of the Victorians which were more theory than fact. I walked again, aimlessly, down the hill.

Joan was sitting on the grass with her legs drawn up, her arms resting on her knees and her face against her arms. She was crying. I had no answer to tears and when I felt an impulse to comfort her, I banished the impulse with an abrupt gesture.

"We better go back to town," I said.

She continued to cry, then she rose slowly, her face turned away from me. She dabbed at her eyes with her handkerchief as she started to walk. I walked behind her, not touching her. Halfway down the hill she stopped.

"I'll never be able to tell you what I feel," she said, "but I want you to know that I am grateful, more grateful than I have ever been to anybody, for anything."

"Everything is all right," I said.

It was a stupid statement but I was not quite tracking in thought or in words. We walked again and when we reached the edge of town the street on which we walked was dark. Joan's voice floated up to me, huskily, not quite steady.

"I did not know that I was like that," she said. "I'm not really. Or I am, I guess. I am glad that you were stronger than I. I want more for myself than I seem able to give myself. I want more for myself than I deserve. I have valued myself, I have respected my life. I—"

She was crying softly again. "You are a human being, Joan," I said. "It is not something that you have to be ashamed of being."

Clumsy sentences seemed to come naturally to me. We reached the clearing before the hotel. All the singers were gone. There were lights in the hotel, only one soft light outside.

"I'll see you in New York," I said.

"We won't even know each other in New York. We'll be different people."

"I'll see you off on your bus tomorrow then, while we still know each other."

"All right." She nodded, then lifted her eyes. Her face was tear-streaked. "All that I can say, Kirk, is thank you," she said.

It was the first time that she had called me "Kirk." I kissed her gently and then I stood there while she walked away from me and into the hotel.

BOOK THREE
The Reality

CHAPTER ONE

Joan's bus to Munich was scheduled to leave at 10 A.M.
There were a great many extra buses because of the play-
goers and some of them were very early. Ten, we had both
agreed when we first discussed the matter, was a sensible
hour in the morning. I was even more in agreement when
I rolled out on Tuesday. I shaved and breakfasted without
any rush or pressure or galloping frenzy. I strolled down to
the bus depot and arrived fifteen minutes early.

There were men and women, a few children, much
luggage and no sign of Joan. Seated on one of the wall
benches was John. He was obviously watching me so I
pretended that I did not see him. He should, certainly, be
at the auditorium, playing his part in the play. He had a
role that ran through the entire play and I wondered how
he could be sitting in the bus station. The why of his
being there was more obvious.

Ten o'clock approached and when it arrived, the bus
doors closed, the engine accelerated and the big vehicle
moved out onto the street. The crowd, that small part of
it that was not on the bus, dissolved. John rose from his
bench and crossed the floor to me.

"She is gone," he said. "She left on the eight o'clock bus.

"How do you know?"

"I was here. She did not say good-bye to me. She did not even speak to me."

"What did you do to her?"

He ignored that question, looking into my face and then away. His eyes were incredibly blue. They seemed to store light rather than merely reflecting it. He was a strikingly handsome young man, taking him feature by feature, but there was something weird in him, something that wiped out the feature-by-feature looks. I could not define that something any more than I could explain the impression that I had of eyes behind his eyes, strange eyes watching me.

The young man interested me less, of course, than Joan. She had left early, deliberately early, to avoid me. There was disappointment in that but no shock. She needed time to put me back in perspective.

"You are an artist," John said. "I have never talked to an artist except to carvers."

"Why aren't you in the play today?"

"I asked my understudy to do it. Will you look at my sculpture in wood?"

"Yes. I would be happy to do so."

It had registered on me that he called other artists in wood "carvers" but considered himself, a sculptor. I doubted that he had waited for me, or had been interested in me, until I considered the obvious. Joan's bus, by his account, had left at eight. He had waited two hours for something.

"I work in the shop of Wilhelm Kistler," he said. "He

is James the Elder in the play. We do not work during the
play. I will show you."

He walked ahead of me, hurrying. There was grace in
him and when one was not engaged in conversation with
him, his beauty returned. I could see his face only in
profile and, quite definitely, he had the look of the Folger
Library Puck. He was, however, older than Puck, older
than he appeared to be in any casual meeting; somewhere,
I would guess, in his early twenties.

The shop was on a side street, on the downtown side
of the church and two blocks away from it. It was a
small shop in a narrow building. There was a laughing
old man, a carving, above the door. The old man was
holding a sign and the sign read: KISTLER. John waved
it away as he was taking his keys from his pocket.

"I ignore that. It is trash," he said. "The father of
Kistler carved it."

I ignored it. The interior of the shop had atmosphere;
two long workbenches, one in the front and one in the
back, a series of shelves on both side walls and armies
of carved figures.

"This bench is mine."

His voice, at that moment, sounded like a child's voice
and when I looked at him he had the appearance of a
child, waiting expectantly for me to praise what was his.

"It is a fine workbench," I said.

He smiled and waved carelessly toward the shelves on
which an assortment of crucifixes, madonnas, bearded
apostles, cherubs, and angels reposed. All of the angels
were playing stringed instruments.

"Many of those carvings I did," he said.

There were two shelves high above his bench, above the

indent shelves which held his tools. He vaulted up easily, standing on the bench to reach what he wanted.

"Here I keep my sculpture."

He handed me an exquisite carving of a Minotaur. The half-bull, half-man stood upright on two legs. The arms and legs were muscular, the arms with hands and the legs with hoofs. The head was that of a beast, a sad-looking bull with large eyes and short horns. The figure was ten inches high and there wasn't a flaw in it. It had been smoothed and waxed and rubbed. I looked at John with new respect. He was standing, relaxed, above me on the bench and he knew that he had earned respect.

"This is a magnificent piece of work," I said. "You are an artist."

"It is mine. I will not sell it."

His lips were tight and I had the idea that someone had wanted him to sell the Minotaur and that there had been conflict about it. He handed down five other carvings, all smaller than the first. There was a weird bird with a beak equal to its height, a naked imp mounted on a horse with a wolf's head, a mask of a bearded man's face, a Griffon, a Centaur.

"What did you use as models," I said.

"I had none. There were pictures of a Minotaur in a book but I changed it. It wasn't correct."

"How do you know?"

"I knew." He jumped down from the bench. "The other creatures I saw."

"Where?"

"I saw them."

I did not argue with him. Imagination is a mysterious gift. I knew that one could see an object existent only within his mind as clearly as he could see a physical object under his hand. I picked up the cavings one by one. It was possible that I was confronted by genius, genius, in the rough, perhaps, but genius.

"It is not enough," John said. "It is limited. One cannot do what one wants to do with wood. I want to sketch and paint. I would give my soul for the things that you have and use."

"It should not be necessary to give your soul for something so simple."

"It is. Would you like to see my secret?"

"What kind of a secret?"

"I will show you."

He was being half a child again but there was, once more, that sense of another presence behind his eyes. He hurried ahead of me to the door, then waited for me so that he could close and lock it. I followed him down streets with very few people. The Passion Play was, of course, in full action.

We went down to the old part of town and my nerves tensed like violin strings when we turned into Kirschbaumstrasse. Here the Lady had walked and here, I had felt, Boniface Rohlmann had lived. John stopped at a doorway half the length of the block, on the side of the street that would have been on the Lady's right, diagonally across from the house with the Jester figure. There was a scar in the wood of the door which indicated that a symbol had been removed; not lately, probably a long time ago. There had been a Griffon between the windows, broken sometime during the years or centuries so that only the front half remained.

"Do you live here?" I asked.

"Yes."

"With whom?"

"My parents."

John opened the door and I followed him into the house.
There was a short hall, a stairway, a parlor off the right
of the hall. The house was quiet, spotlessly clean and
obviously not a home of wealth or position. The parents,
whatever they did normally, probably worked at the auditorium during the Passion Play or at temporary jobs
created by the influx of tourists.

"I will get them," John said. "I have to hide them."

He was obviously referring to the secrets that he had
mentioned, not to his parents. "Why do you have to hide
them?" I said.

"They will not let me do what I want to do."

"Who won't let you?"

"My parents. Kistler. Everybody."

He waved me into the parlor and took the stairs two
at a time. The parlor was stiff, not unfriendly but obviously
not at ease with a stranger. There was a large portrait on
the south wall, the portrait of a belligerent old man with
an inflated mustache. Facing him from the other wall was
a self-conscious old woman with her hair drawn back into
a bun. Ancestors. The furniture was old, uninspired, each
piece placed uncompromisingly in the spot assigned to
it.

John came back. He had white cards in his hand, the
4″×6″ and 3″×5″ cards that one can buy in a dime
store or a stationery shop in the United States. He held
them for a few seconds then thrust them toward me. I
took them and walked to the window with them. A surprising amount of light flowed into the room despite the
draperies. It was a tall window.

He had sketched on those cards. He had had only the
cheapest, most ordinary pencil. He had had the crayons

of a child and he had recognized the inadequacy of those. Only a few of his sketches had color.

There was an ugly dwarf sitting on a curved piece of stone that was like an overturned arch from a church portal. The dwarf had his legs drawn up and his long-toed feet were bare. He had an oversized hand resting against the side of his face, shielding it from view. There was a squat, bearded man with an upraised ax and two gross rodents facing each other. There was a bat in flight. There was a four-legged reptile with a man's face, a face of down-drawn mouth and bulging eyes. There were two sketches of naked men running and one of a nude male with his arms raised high. There was a sketch of the outdoor Saint Krispin, the one with the "K," and one sketch of Saint George and the Dragon.

It was all very young work, amateur work, and the sketch of Saint George and Company was definitely bad. I did not hold that against John because there were shudderingly bad paintings of that subject in good museums with good names attached to them. I lifted my eyes and John was crouched, tensely crouched, watching me. My looking at the pictures obviously meant much to him and he read more in my face than I wanted to reveal.

"You do not believe that they are good?" he said. "They are not art?" He came out of his crouch and his arms dropped. "I have no materials. I have no tools."

"Why not? You have materials and tools for carving."

"They let me carve. They will not let me sketch. I want to paint. I am not permitted."

I glanced down again at the sketches. They were all of men. There was not one of a woman. There were no Passion Play traces, no sacred pictures, no saints but Krispin. John had a nice sense of line and a seemingly instinctive knowledge of anatomy, probably a by-product of his carving. His instinct for perspective, too, was good but characters in motion, such as the running men, were a bit beyond him yet.

"Have you seen any great paintings?" I said. "Visited any museums?"

"None. I went once to Munich but they would not let me go to the museum."

The power and the authority of "they" seemed beyond belief. It seemed arbitrary and out of all reason to forbid museums and great art and the simple tools of sketching to someone who ached to be a painter. Only one trip to Munich in his lifetime, the great city only a few hours away! John was sitting on one of the lightly upholstered chairs, staring at me, aware that he had my interest, waiting. He was less childish now than he had been but the childishness was there and the something that hid behind his eyes and the something that carved monsters and sketched odd men.

Judas had said that there were children who remained children even though their bodies became adult. He did not go into too many particulars but, seemingly, a village as old as this one was a repository of folklore. Everything had happened before and for all ontoward things there were remedies. The village accepted John into its life as a man, granted him the respected art of creating images in wood, gave him an honored place in its play, but held him under authority as it held children. The old and the wise approved his assuming the role of guide and companion to a girl but, obviously, would deny him the same role with a strange man. They might have been right. I did not know.

"Let us take a walk, John," I said.

"Why?"

"I have to think about something. I think better when I walk."

He took the cards from me and went upstairs with them. I was interested in the house. It had, of course, been changed, reconditioned, painted, during the centuries and one would not be able to trace back through the changes to anything vital. Houses, like people, had their own secrets and preserved them. It would be pointless of me to walk through the house or to see the rooms of it. If it meant anything to me in the seeing, the meaning that I drew from it might be utterly misleading.

This was one of the shadowy indistinct houses behind the house with the unicorn that Boniface Rohlmann painted with the Lady. It might be the house in which he lived, included in his painting as identity of a sort but denied top prominence out of modesty or out of decent reticence.

I could almost hear the house breathing in the silence. Arbitrarily I had decided that the house of the Jester was the house of Boniface Rohlmann. Why not this house? On the same street, and in his painting as the Jester house was not, this house was more logically the house in which he was born, grew up, made his first experiments in sketching. The room in which I stood was a room in which someone had stood or paced during those grim days and nights of the Black Death when the crude wagon banged through the streets to the pit. Why could not that person have been a Rohlmann?

John came back. He looked discontented, rebellious, childish. He had wanted me to stay there in the house; perhaps find something in his work and discuss it. I could understand all of that and sympathize with it but staying in the house was not an answer.

We walked to the end of Kirschbaumstrasse and turned left. I led him to the old plague pit and he was still sulking, leaving it to me to open any conversational lead. The pit field was peaceful, a flat barren space that had known horror and that slept now forgetting it.

"John," I said, "do you know anything about Boniface Rohlmann?"

"Who?"

"Boniface Rohlmann."

"No. Who was he?"

"Someone who lived in this town a long time ago."

"I never heard of him."

That settled one vague question in my mind. There had been the chance that Rohlmann was better known to the people of Freidheim than anyone had admitted to me. There was no doubting John, however. The name meant nothing to him and he was indifferent.

"What would you do with equipment like mine if you had it?" I said.

"I would copy pictures. I would learn, copying. There are pictures at the auditorium."

"Painting is not easy. You would have to learn many things, work very hard."

"I know. It is not easy to sculpt in wood."

He had pride in his voice. He knew how good he was. He might have to go back to beginnings, down to fundamentals but he understood that need. He was already an artist.

There was a touch of irony in the thought that this young sculptor wanted to paint, seeking a higher art while I, who painted, was obsessed by the work of sculptors.

I wanted to give this young man the pencils and the

boards and the paper that I had with me. I was not certain
that I had the right to do so. He was of this village and
the village, for reasons of its own and for what it saw
in him, did not want him to have the tools or the
materials of an artist. The village might know best or it
might not. That Minotaur, if one discounted everything
else, was a tremendous piece of work. I had felt, looking
at it, that I might be in the presence of genius. This
youth had had no art study, no museums, no access to
what others had learned in the field of painting but he
wanted to paint. He had made his own start under fantastic
difficulty. Given the chance, might he not put on canvas
something as good as that Minotaur? Better?

It was like one of the debates about right and wrong,
good and evil. I was an artist, not a philosopher, and
there was, in the end, only one way I could decide the
question.

"John," I said, "I am going to give you all the material
that I have with me; pencils, boards, paper. Can you take
care of them?"

He stopped in midstride and stood straight. He looked
at me and there was something frightening in his face,
frightening because it held an emotion that I had never
encountered, an emotion moving in his features, his eyes.
He did not speak and did not attempt to speak. He was
the one who needed to walk now and he walked. I followed him.

This was what a truly great want was like, how it
looked. I had never felt so great a want even when I was
priding myself on feeling or on control of feeling. This,
perhaps, in one face was the definition of genius if one
could read it.

I had wondered about Joan, how she could be so in-
fatuated with so obvious a child. I understood now. He
had not been a child when he was with her. She was
new, different, and she had called out something from
that deeper something inside him. She had been charmed
by him and reassured by the absence of masculine drive
or demand in him, not understanding the reason for the
absence. This John could be many things. I could only
guess at what he had been, in the end, with her.

"I am not certain that I am doing the right thing," I
said. "I am giving my things to an artist, not to a man.
Understand that! If I mailed something to you from Munich
would you get it?"

"When?"

"Tomorrow when I reach there."

"Yes. The shop. Kistler. I will watch for them."

He gave me the address and I wrote it down. There was
no saying of thanks. He was someone to whom the impossible had happened and he was still stunned. We came
to the Bahnhof, as quiet as the rest of the town.

"Wait here by the fountain," I said. "I'll bring the
stuff down."

The clerk at the desk in the hotel stopped me. He had
a note in a small envelope. I opened the envelope when
I reached my room. The script was fine, beautifully formed
letters in straight marching lines:

*Kirk—I am taking the early bus. Cowardly maybe. I do
not know at this minute. I couldn't talk to you this morning.
I do not remember what I said last night, something inadequate. The thing that I wanted to tell you, I guess, is
that you saved me from being a mere episode. I am grateful*

to you for that, forever grateful. It was not easy for you, I know. Am I incoherent? Probably so. Anyway, Kirk, if we are different people in New York, as we will be, I am glad that we knew each other in Friedheim. I will remember us.

Joan.

There was not time to think about the note. I read it and held it in my hand and it was, somehow, the portrait of a person. I could sympathize with her strong resistance to becoming a mere episode in another person's life. I had lived through that. I had been an episode once.

I shook my head and came reluctantly back to John.

There were no more sketches to make in Friedheim and I could buy more paper, pencils, boards, color, and the rest of it when I got away. I had no paper in which to wrap my gear and it had to be protected, from damage and from curious or disapproving eyes. It took a bit of mental wrestling but, in the end, I moved my notes and sketches into my suitcase and gave my dispatch case as a carrier to John.

There was a man talking to John when I came out of the hotel, a stern, bearded man who was shaking his finger to emphasize whatever he was saying. It did not seem to be a friendly discourse so I avoided any involvement in it. I walked to the shop with the sign that said KISTLER and, after a momentary hesitation, laid my dispatch case down against the door.

John was alone when I walked back but now that the vigilant town had discovered his presence, the fact that an understudy was playing his role in the auditorium, I did not expose him to the risk of conversation.

"I left the material at the door of Kistler," I said. "It is in a black case. Keep the case, and good luck!"

I went back into the hotel and the church bell rang. It was lunchtime. The crowd would be pouring back from the auditorium.

There were many things that I could have done with my afternoon, the last afternoon in Friedheim. I elected to write up my notes; the heard, the observed, the remembered. I always have had the ability to separate fact and interpretation, putting them in separate boxes. I did not let myself relax with the interpretation of my facts until the dark came down and I was in my room for the night.

In the end I had found what I had never had a hope of finding. I had found Boniface Rohlmann.

He was, of course—must have been—such a youth as John Veit. In the wake of plague and invasion, he had had no more opportunity in the beginning than had John; no museums, no art, no anything. The genius, certainly, was there and, I was positive of it, the odd something that was in John. The village might have tried to protect him, too, but it was a difficult time and the boy had slipped away. He had, some way and somehow, known Italy and the work of Tintoretto and Caravaggio. Were there such opposite poles as Good and Evil? Rohlmann gained the opportunity to paint. He was a great painter. In gaining the opportunity, in developing his tremendous power, he was misunderstood. His work vanished. His hope of fame dissolved and he burned at the stake. Maybe he dealt with sorcery and sorcerers. A thousand maybes!

Today I had walked on Kirschbaumstrasse with John Veit. It was like walking that street with Boniface Rohlmann, the street that he had painted. I had the feeling that this youth looked as Rohlmann had looked. Why had his parents and the elders banned painting for him and permitted sculpture in wood? Where all the records had been lost, was there some thread of memory in a village, a thread that people touched without understanding?

"A man could go crazy on a merry-go-round like that," I said.

The night was cloudy outside of my narrow little windows. I was tired but just before I crossed the line to sleep, Alicia walked through my life again. She often did but she never stayed long; she merely strolled out of a memory and went back again.

A friend of hers had died during the early months of our marriage and Alicia, with no smallest religious or philosophical streak in her, went to the rosary for him at some Catholic church at the other end of town.

"Why?" I said.

She did not know, of course. "I hope that he is somewhere," she said. "I hate to think of him as being not."

I had often remembered that remark. I remembered it when I had the phone call telling me that Alicia had driven her automobile off a mountain road in California. The police listed it as an accident. I flew to California and I paid for the funeral. Max Henske did not even attend it. I was the only mourner because it was the wrong coast and, somehow, I did not mourn for her.

"I hope that he is somewhere. I hate to think of him as being not."

I remembered that now but I thought of Boniface Rohlmann. It was a summing up.

CHAPTER TWO

Munich in a few hours was a confusion of people, a sense of sparkle and excitement, of well-being and good weather. London, in a day and a night, was much the same; familiar buildings in familiar settings, new buildings of appalling ugliness, a walk up Charing Cross Road from Trafalgar Square, visiting bookshops on the way. I was out of London in the morning and the Atlantic from an airplane is something to be endured. At the end of it was New York.

My time schedule was shattered. Nothing happened in the right segment of the day; breakfast, lunch, drinktime, or dinner seemed in the wrong slots. In a time sense I was a European, operating by European clocks. I wanted to see Ludwig Lorenson before I saw anyone else but I could not even come up to the point of calling him on the phone.

My mail, for the most part, was innocuous. There were bills to be paid, little else. A long, pleasant-looking envelope from *Sphere* contained a check, a larger check than I expected, more money than they would have paid the German photographer if he had trailed Joan Terrill through all of her hours. I walked around my studio apartment, looking at things, letting them slowly become real to me again. There was work that I had left unfinished and none of it seemed important. A book that I had been reading was on my desk, a page marker indicating where I had stopped. I could not remember what the book had been about so it made no difference where I had stopped.

Full circle brought me back to the check. I remembered Joan's promise that she would make *Sphere* pay me for my work and the lack of confidence in her voice. I remembered, too, her exuberance, her happiness, when she came into my hotel with the cable from *Sphere* in her hand. I picked up the bulky Manhattan telephone book and turned the pages slowly, not totally committed to them. I found the Terrills and she had her own phone. I assured myself that she would not be home but I dialed the number and listened to two rings before her voice came on the line.

"This is Herr Gustave von Schultz," I said in German, "Of the Geiger Hotel! The hotel is distressed that you left behind you a glove. They have sent me to return it to you."

"Oh!" Her voice caught and I could, literally, see her fingers opening and closing, reaching for something. *"Ja!"* Her voice let her down and she went into English. "Dammit, I can't do it," she said. "I wish that I was an actress. I'm just a square. I can't do these things. Where are you?"

"On a hillside sketching a cow."

She did not miss that. "Oh! You haven't changed, then?"

"No. How about you?"

"Yes. Oh, yes. I am certain that I have. Maybe not importantly. I don't know."

"We'll find out. Are you busy tonight?"

"No. What time?"

"Seven. I'll pick you up. Your place. We'll find a first-class delicatessen somewhere."

"Yes. I'll like that. Seven."

She was not a poised girl when there was no research project on which to lean. One could throw her off balance with a finger tip of pressure. She would not always be like that, of course. Women found their centers of balance so much easier than did men. She wished that she was an actress. Lord! If she had even a drop of actress blood in her veins I would not even talk to her on the telephone.

Thought of the telephone confronted me once again with my realities. Ludwig knew when I was due to arrive. He would not expect an immediate call but he would feel ignored if he had to wait too long. I looked at the phone, feeling alien to it, then dialed his number. Ludwig's voice was cool, detached, professional.

"Kirk? It is good to have you in this country again. How is your time?"

"Mixed up. You, however, are the only concern occupying it.

"Excellent. I will see you then. A half hour?"

"Make it three quarters. I'll walk."

"Walk briskly. I'll be waiting."

Once I was committed to something I felt at home. I took Ludwig's advice and walked briskly but the city astonished me. It had vanished, disappeared completely, and it was back again; all around me, noise and smoke and odor, hurrying people. Something within me shrank from it but I knew that the rhythm would pick me up again and that I would accept this as the world, all else an unreality.

The Lorenson Galleries were aloof from people in passage, dignified, bearing the look of the exclusive, the expensive, the rare. There was a new elevator man, a Negro of light skin, a man of reserve whose only interest in me was the fact that I wanted the fourth floor.

The fourth floor was as it had always been, and why not? I had been gone only a short time, a very short time. Ludwig rose from his desk to meet me. He had lost some weight and the pouches under his eyes were more pronounced. He smiled and held out his hand.

"Kirk, the trip agreed with you. You look splendid. I wish that I had gone along."

"I wish you had, too. I am not certain that you would have liked Friedheim."

"I would have hated the place. I dislike small towns, even in this country. I am in your debt for letters. I never write any."

"There were things I wanted to tell you."

"You told them well. There are other things?"

"I am afraid not. Nothing significant."

We were facing each other across his desk. The Antonello da Messina scoundrel looked down upon us from the wall. A charming scoundrel! There was a faint fragrance in the room. I had not told Ludwig of John Veit. He would not have been interested. He would not have been interested in the parish priest of Friedheim, either, nor in Joan Terrill.

"You did not discover anything about that painter, Rohlmann."

"A small painting in the church. I told you in a letter."

"A Madonna. Early work. Yes. Nothing else?"

"He died in Friedheim, not Trier. You knew that yourself. You didn't tell me."

"Information can be error. One collects much of it and sorts what he collects."

"Rohlmann lived on Kirschbaumstrasse in Friedheim, a one block street."

"So!" Ludwig smiled. "You are writing his life?"

"No."

"So, none of that is any good to you."

"Very little. Can you tell me more?"

Ludwig shook his head. His interest in Boniface Rohlmann as a person and as a painter had always been small. He sat with his fingertips together, looking at me, and I knew that all the polite preliminaries were over. He might have hoped that I would stumble on some lost lode of old paintings, or on a lead to them, but the hope could never have been strong. If he had a number of Rohlmanns he would be interested in the painter, but only then.

"That painting which inspired your journeying has a bad history," he said. "The papers that came with it to me said that it had caused trouble wherever shown and that the painter escaped death in Trier by hiding in the home of someone known to my friends in Würzburg." Ludwig spread his hands apart. "There, perhaps, is where your rumor started, the rumor that this Rohlmann was burned in Trier. No matter. The painting has trouble in it, grave trouble. It cannot be exhibited." His mouth tightened. "It has cost me three friends."

"I cannot believe that you have lost Neil Carlton."

"He has lost me. No matter. I have made a decision. It is, for me, a hard decision. I have lost sleep over it. The decision is made. I shall exhibit that painting no more. I shall burn it as this Friedheim burned the painter."

"No. You can't."

"I can. It is mine. I own it."

"No one owns a piece of art. One is a custodian. Never more than that."

"It is not art. It is something evil. It must be destroyed."

"Ludwig," I said. "I have to see it again. I must."

He looked at me for a long minute, a half smile on his face. "This I knew, that you would want to see it when you came from this Friedheim. It is in your mind. I lost three friends. Of the four who saw the picture, you alone remain. You wrote me letters, long letters. You are my friend. If you want to see that painting again, you shall see it. You are the last."

"Thank you, Ludwig."

I felt rather ill as I followed him down the long passage but anticipation lifted me as Ludwig snapped the light switch in the same monastically severe room in which I had first seen the painting.

Nothing had changed. The large canvas floated upon the light which flowed in under it. Ludwig turned his back to it. I was aware of that, then Ludwig and all else faded from my awareness, all else save the scene before me.

I was standing beside the low east wall of a courtyard with the pale morning sun at my back. There were angry human beings in the courtyard and Roman soldiers seeking to drive a path through them. There was a solitary figure in mid-courtyard, black clouds in the northwest, wind blowing the garments of the people, rippling the water in a series of puddles. The figure of the solitary man dominated the scene in which so many people moved.

Jesus Christ, standing in the center of the courtyard, looked as he had looked in Friedheim. He wore a white robe stained with blood and he stood straight with obvious effort, his legs apart. He had been beaten and he was dazed.

There was a crowd shouting at him and hurling missiles, but he was a figure of tremendous dignity. I found it difficult to look away from him.

The mob was like mobs anywhere; hysterical, emotional, unthinking, cruel. It was an arc of people here, giving way reluctantly under the pressure of Roman soldiery. I looked reluctantly for myself. I was not there. The cowardly, sneaky creature who stooped for a stone to throw from his safe position behind the crowd, was just that, a despicable stranger. I was no longer in the painting.

I blinked and looked again. This was just a mob, a beautifully painted mob, as alive as the actors in Friedheim and more real. Then I saw *her*.

She was in the second row of that rabble; Joan Terrill, her face contorted with hatred, her hand drawn back. She was about to throw her stone at the defenseless man who stood inside the semicircle of Romans. This was the sweet-faced, insecure religious girl who had wept at the Passion Play. She was as rabidly furious as the rest of them, as mindlessly stirred to hatred. I heard the voice of Friedheim's priest dimly in my mind.

"You are a sinner. I have no doubt of it. I have never met a man who was not."

I had recognized the truth of that when I heard him speak, so why should I be surprised to find anyone I knew in that screaming mob? I was still staring at Joan. By whatever magic was in the picture, whether it be calling on a mind projection from the viewer or something else, I did not know why I should be seeing her. I could hear her voice as I had heard the priest's.

"I wanted only one ultimate person," she said, "one ultimate experience. I was willing to wait. I could not be casual."

"She is the other half of myself," I said.

I did not know that I had spoken aloud. Ludwig turned his head. "What? What did you say?"

"You cannot burn that painting, Ludwig!" I said.

He snapped the switch and the painting vanished. "You are my friend," he said, "but you cannot tell me what I can, or cannot, do."

He walked ahead of me down the corridor, a heavy man despite his recent loss of weight. His heels hit hard. When we entered his study he was prepared to say goodbye to me, making no motion toward his chair or his desk.

"If you burn that painting, Ludwig," I said, "you will be acting like that big stupid Roman. He doesn't know why he is pushing the people back. He doesn't care. You do not know whether someone in ten years, or fifty, will understand that painting and discover more about the painter. No! Just let's burn it. It is easier than understanding."

"Don't Don't say that! I stayed awake nights, thinking about burning it. I have never wanted to burn anything. That big Roman, that brute with the sword! It made me sick to see my face on him."

"I remember," I said.

Ludwig walked around his desk and dropped heavily into his chair. "The thing is evil. What do you want me to do, perpetuate it?"

"No. You do not know that it is evil. You do not know what evil is, or if there is evil. All I want is for you to preserve that painting. It is one of the world's great paintings."

"Preserve how? For what? Where? It cannot be exhibited."

I sat in the chair facing him. I did not want Ludwig to lose another friend because of that painting. I did not want to lose a friend myself. It was a tense moment.

"Ludwig," I said, "if that painting belongs anywhere in the world, it is in Friedheim. The only other existent painting of Boniface Rohlmann is there. Rohlmann's dust is out in the plague pit."

"A small German town could not afford such a painting."

"No. And you cannot afford to sell it. There is a priest who preserved the other Rohlmann. Maybe he can do something for this. If it can, now or someday, be shown, it is the benevolence of Ludwig Lorenson, the great gift. If the town burns it as it burned Boniface Rohlmann, it is not your burning."

Ludwig Lorenson's eyes were intent upon my face. He sat straight in his chair and command of the conversation moved softly back to him before he spoke a word. I felt that passing of command without defining it. He rose slowly.

"I will think on this, Kirk," he said.

I knew then that I had won my point as I knew that Ludwig needed time to reach his own decision in a way that would not be an adopting of mine. He walked with me to the elevator door, and, for a moment, his hand rested on my shoulder.

"You were away a short time," he said. "You have grown, matured. There is much of the year left. I want to see the paintings that you will do in it."

"You will see them, Ludwig," I said.

The elevator took me down under the quiet detached guidance of the operator whom I did not know, whose name I did not know. There was a hushed, dignified silence in the gallery downstairs and a bedlam of sound in the street. I walked south.

I had to see Neil Carlton, Ultimately I would see Joan. There was much of a year ahead of me, Ludwig said. Yes. And much of a lifetime ahead of me, with all the unwritten and the unpainted and the unspoken. The bustling, hustling, pushing horde of people picked me up and hurried me along. I was home.